MW01688208

GOLDIE'S DAUGHTER

BONNIE DODGE

booktrope

Booktrope Editions
Seattle, WA 2015

Cover Design by Greg Simanson
Edited by Barbara Brannon

This is a work of fiction. Names, characters, places, brands, media, and incidents are either the product of the author's imagination or are used fictitiously. Any resemblance to similarly named places or to persons living or deceased is unintentional.

PRINT ISBN 978-1-5137-0322-0
EPUB ISBN 978-1-5137-0330-5
Library of Congress Control Number: 2015914518

Back East there is a better life,
No digging in the dirt,
Or staring in a miner's pan
Until your eyelids hurt.
A place where parasols are made
Of Paris silk so fine,
A place where steamboats paddle by,
A place that I'd call mine.
Back East is where I wish to go—
I'd like to run away
From all these mountains, trees, and chores.
Back East is where I'd stay.
Somewhere there is another sky
That's just this shade of blue,
Somewhere back East, away from here,
Where all your dreams come true.

Emily Ann McIntyre
Sawtooth City
April 29, 1882

CHAPTER ONE

"It's nothing," returned Mrs. Chick. "It's merely change of weather. We must expect change."
Charles Dickens, DOMBEY AND SON

EMILY'S STRAW MATTRESS, tucked in a corner on the floor, rustled as she shifted her weight and leaned toward the window, squinting to see which birds were responsible for the early morning disturbance. It was still dark outside, not quite dawn, and the only thing Emily could see was shadows. She glanced toward the moon, but that too was obscured. A cloud cover hid the morning stars. When she inhaled, she smelled disquietude as surely as she smelled rain.

She pulled her thin wool blanket closer to her chin and shivered. She was growing too tall for the covers, much less the skimpy mattress tick. Soon it was quiet outside, so quiet all Emily could hear were children breathing. She glanced to where her charges shared a bed. George had kicked his covers free and turned toward the wall. Lizzie was curled in the shape of a comma, with her pillow scrunched into a ball and cradled close like a doll. Emily listened to their steady, even breathing and wondered if they would feel it, this restlessness that seemed to have invaded Saw Tooth Valley, Idaho Territory, like a fever.

If she were superstitious, she would have been wary, careful of the uneasy stirrings winter left behind. But Emily was old enough to know there were no superstitions left in the Saw Tooth Mountains. Only cold, tired men chasing dreams with gold pans, shovels, and picks. Soon they would be flooding the valley again like spring rains, greedy army ants in search of gold and silver.

Even if George and Lizzie didn't feel the restlessness, Emily did. Even the birds sensed it—woke her early then hushed—waiting, nervous and uneasy as the day grew lighter. As minutes pattered by like raindrops, birds squawked to each other and ruffled their feathers, anticipating something more than the promise of spring and full bellies.

Emily yawned and peered out the window. Then she pushed away the unwanted feeling, the unwanted restiveness that entered Saw Tooth Valley in the spring of 1882, the same way she pushed back her wool blanket. With a tired sigh, she began another day.

* * *

"Hold still!" Emily struggled to pull a comb through Lizzie's thick dark curls and secured the unruly tresses with a new pink ribbon. "There." Emily stepped back and admired. "You look just like Alice in Wonderland."

Lizzie giggled, then pouted. "Wish you were coming with us."

Emily scrunched up her face, making Lizzie giggle even harder. "You know I can't. Now get moving."

Lizzie exaggerated her pout until her bottom lip protruded. She even found a way to make it quiver. "But I'll miss you. You have the prettiest voice in the whole world."

"How would you know that, Miss Harmon? Have you seen the whole world? Besides, I have work to do." That was no exaggeration—Emily had her usual morning chores to tend to, plus readying the extra sleeping rooms for the Kerry Chapman Troupe, scheduled to arrive that very day.

Eight years old and bored beyond patience, George poked his head through the doorway and tossed his make-believe curls. "Look at me, I'm *sooooo* pretty."

"Oh, you!" Lizzie turned to chase her brother but stopped short, just in time to prevent a collision with her mother. Harriet Harmon entered the kitchen wearing her best Sunday suit, a double-breasted royal blue woolen with tiny silk buttons. Emily stepped back, out of the way, while Mrs. Harmon straightened Lizzie's pink bow and inspected her son's usually dirty ears. She looked at her children with pride, and Emily couldn't help but wish that once, just once, Mrs. Harmon would look at her with the same regard.

"Nice job, George," Mrs. Harmon said. "Now hurry. We don't want to be late. Reverend Kingsley so very rarely gets to Saw Tooth City." Mrs. Harmon hustled her children toward the front door, where her stout husband tapped his gold-tipped cane impatiently against the wooden floor. She pulled her parasol from the new hall tree, a piece so new the smell of freshly sawn oak still lingered in the air. With a nod to Emily, Mrs. Harmon said, "We should be back by one."

As a way of asserting his authority, Mr. Harmon added, "And I expect dinner to be ready when we return." Emily's guardian donned his felt hat and pushed his family out the door, as if staying in the room near Emily was more than he could manage. Which, if the rumors that he killed Emily's father in a dispute over a mining claim were true, was warranted. She didn't trust him, but as his ward she knew her options were limited. She continued to tell herself the gossips weren't truthful, the same way she told George and Lizzie about elves and Santa Claus.

Apparently unaware of her husband's discomfort, Mrs. Harmon took his arm, and the smartly dressed family walked down the gravel road toward the new town hall. Emily watched from the doorway until she could no longer see them. Dragging herself to the kitchen, she filled the sink with hot water and sang the ditty she'd composed while trying to sleep some nights. *Back East there is a better life*…abruptly, she stopped her song. Let them go off to church, dressed in their Sunday best, Mrs. Harmon's stays so tight she could hardly breathe. There were more important things to do than parade around town in new clothes. Just what, Emily couldn't quite say, but she knew there had to be more to living than washing dishes, having babies, and dressing up just to strut down the rutty street of a dirty mining camp.

Any other time her curiosity would have prompted her to finish her work early, allowing her to accompany the Harmons to hear the Reverend Kingsley preach. But Emily wasn't sure she wanted to sit in a room full of pious people with one or two sure to look her way when the preacher warned against temptation, sin, and damnation. Not when she already felt so restless and out of sorts.

Just last week she was tempted, was even caught peeking at Mrs. Harmon's latest copy of *Harper's Bazaar* when she should have been dusting the furniture in the parlor. "What's that you're looking at?" Mrs. Harmon had said, and Emily almost tipped over an expensive glass pitcher in her attempt to conceal the magazine.

Emily had hid the issue, quickly closing the pages on young women in white linen dresses shaded by pale silk parasols as they watched steamboats travel up and down the Mississippi River. Emily studied the pictures, hungry for adventure. What she wouldn't give to be aboard one of those steamboats, floating lazily down the Mississippi. Somewhere. Anywhere. Somewhere far away from these mountains, where no one would know her.

Or know about her mother.

When the kitchen was neat and the dishes put away, Emily gathered her cleaning supplies and headed for the bedrooms upstairs. In the guest suite she plumped feather pillows and smoothed the down comforter over the mattress, wishing her own bed was this nice. Usually she was grateful for her adequate room and board, but today the thought of sleeping on an old straw mattress made her angry. If she could, she'd change her name to Alice, and, like the girl in the book, follow the white rabbit straight away from Saw Tooth City. But her name was Emily, and the only place she was going was to work.

She punched the pillow. The warm spring wind had blown something else besides Reverend Kingsley into the thawing alpine valley. Something that stirred longings deep inside her; something that made her feet itch and her mind wander. She crossed the room and opened the window. The rain had stopped, leaving the valley wet and shiny. A breeze billowed the white lace curtain and filled the bedroom with the smell of warm dirt, wet pine, and melting snow. Emily pressed her nose against the ledge of the window until she saw the robin, twittering in a tree below. She watched, transfixed, until the bird opened its wings and flew away.

Later, when the Harmons returned from church, the first thing Mrs. Harmon did was hand Emily her bonnet and ask, "Is dinner ready?"

Emily jiggled the plumes on the hat, watching the blue spikes wave back and forth like some silly bird shaking dust from its tail feathers. Before she could answer, Lizzie proclaimed, "Oh, Emily, it was wonderful. You should have been there. They brought in Mrs. Belden's new parlor organ and we sang and sang." In her excitement, Lizzie knocked the bonnet from Emily's hands when she leaned closer and whispered, "But no one sings as good as you."

Emily retrieved the hat, hoping Mrs. Harmon hadn't noticed it drop to the floor. "Go!" She spun Lizzie toward the kitchen. "Be sure to wash those hands good and hard now. Scoot."

George, imitating his father's actions, hung his cap on an iron peg on the oak hall tree. Back straight with newfound importance, he headed for the dining room. But Emily stopped him. "George, you too."

George scowled but followed his sister into the kitchen. Soon the family had taken their places around the dining room table. As usual, Emily was seated at the table near the door so she could run to the kitchen for more food or water if needed.

"Everything looks lovely, Emily." Mrs. Harmon ladled generous servings of green beans for her children, filled her own plate, and handed the empty platter back to Emily. "I do wish Reverend Kingsley could have joined us for dinner. We would have insisted, but he has services to attend to this evening in Vienna."

Emily set aside the empty platter and listened quietly as Mrs. Harmon continued.

"The community was very generous, didn't you think, Gideon? I hope the collection was enough to encourage him to return soon. We could use our own church and reverend, this town is growing so fast."

"You heard what Pierson said." Mr. Harmon tipped his forkful of roast beef toward her. "If we get a full-time preacher, Abe won't be able to keep the saloon open on Sundays."

"It wouldn't hurt to incorporate a bit of civilization into this town," Mrs. Harmon bantered.

"Next thing, you'll be wanting to bring that Anthony woman here." Mr. Harmon sawed at the meat on his plate and Emily watched in silence, afraid she might have overcooked the roast again.

Mrs. Harmon ignored his remark. "Jane Belden offered to give Lizzie music lessons."

"Oh, can I, Papa?"

"We'll see." Mr. Harmon turned to his son. "I'm going to need your help with firewood this afternoon. We'll want a good amount ready before the guests arrive."

George nodded, his mouth full of potatoes.

"I can help," Lizzie offered. "Please, Papa?"

"We'll see." Mr. Harmon lifted his glass toward Emily. "Emily, where's that lemonade?"

Emily fetched the pitcher from the sideboard and filled his glass. "Did you hear any more about the troupe?" she asked, setting the pitcher back on the sideboard.

"No," Mrs. Harmon answered for him. "No one seems to know when to expect them."

As Emily circled the table, removing dinner plates and replacing them with dessert bowls filled with canned peaches, she said, "The handbill in Mr. Belden's window said the troupe has an excellent reputation in Portland and Sacramento. And Jenny Starr is so pretty, don't you think?"

"I hardly think so. After all, she's . . ." Mrs. Harmon pushed her fruit aside, as if she'd suddenly lost her appetite. "In any event, it will be nice to have the boarding house full of people again." She rose to leave the room.

"God knows we could use the revenue." Mr. Harmon folded his napkin and dropped it by his plate. He turned to his son. "George, we have work to do." Lizzie looked at her father expectantly, but he ignored her. "Change your clothes and meet me outdoors," he instructed the boy.

As soon as Mr. Harmon and George left the room, Emily slid into the chair beside Lizzie. Together they finished the last of the peaches. It was only later, when Emily was alone with Mrs. Harmon in the kitchen, that she dared ask, "Do you think I could see the performance?"

"We'll see," Mrs. Harmon parroted her husband.

We'll see, Emily thought as she watched Mrs. Harmon leave the kitchen. *May just as well say no. Bet my real mother wouldn't say no. Bet my real mother would even take me.* Emily blushed at the thought, knowing that if her real mother were there to take her, they wouldn't be able to walk down the street without drawing whispers, let alone take in a lively theatrical like the one the Kerry Chapman Troupe had advertised. But that didn't keep Emily from wanting to go.

Emily dried the last of the glasses and put the dishes in the cupboard. Picking up her sewing, she went outside to sit on the porch, where the sun was warm against her face. She tilted her head up, closed her eyes, and inhaled. Instead of the fresh pine-scent of spring she expected, she inhaled dust and sneezed. She scowled at the road. With the harsh winter storms behind them, Saw Tooth City was booming with newcomers arriving every day. Even now, another miner leading a string of mules sauntered down Main Street toward the saloon, stirring up clouds of alkali dust. Oh, what she wouldn't give for the paved streets she read about in Mrs. Harmon's magazines. Streets made with cobblestones and bricks like the ones back East or in St. Louis instead of this ugly crushed granite and dust. Coughing, Emily turned her attention to her sewing, hemming lace to the bottom of a new dress for Lizzie. When finished, she held the dress up and admired the stitches, so small they were barely visible.

She glanced at her own dress, plain in comparison. Too tight, the gray fabric pulled across her chest; the sleeves stopped several inches above her wrists. She must have grown a good twelve inches over winter. Tucking her legs under the bench, Emily knew it would take more than lace to hide the fact that her dress was now too short, fully unacceptable for a girl her age. She sighed and lay back against the porch. When she was sure no one was watching, Emily reached into her pocket and pulled out the handbill Mr. Belden had given her with yesterday's grocery purchases.

"Hang this in your window," he had instructed, but Emily had kept the flyer instead, secretly reading it every chance she dared. Now she unfolded the paper and reread the seductive words. "Don't miss the Kerry Chapman Troupe. The finest performance west of the Mississippi."

Emily memorized the picture of Jenny Starr, the leading lady's dark hair pulled up and pinned to cascade down her back in ringlets, a pretty heart-shaped locket lying close to her bosom. With her finger, Emily traced the word Mississippi. Then she ran inside and located the atlas Mr. Harmon kept in the parlor. Having no idea where to look for the river, Emily turned page after page after page. She was ready to give up when, there, in the middle of a map of the

United States, she found it. She followed the line that began in Minnesota and ended in the Gulf of Mexico, dividing the country in two. Over and over she traced the river until her fingertip turned inky blue.

Returning the atlas to the parlor, Emily closed her eyes and made a wish.

CHAPTER TWO

"I only ask to be free. The butterflies are free."
BLEAK HOUSE

IF WISHES CAME TRUE, Emily would be boarding a train headed east, straight for the Mississippi River. It was all she'd thought about for more than a week now, disappointed but still hopeful as she waited for the overdue Chapman troupe to arrive in Saw Tooth City. Her handbill was tattered, worn to pieces from too much folding and unfolding. She looked at the pamphlet so many times she had every word memorized, every image etched in her soul. Yet she continued to open and close it, as if by simply touching the paper, she could make the troupe miraculously appear.

But wishes were only dreams conjured up somewhere between the heart and the head—where, Emily wasn't quite sure. So every night she pored over Mr. Harmon's atlas until she had that page, the one where the Mississippi River divided America in two, memorized also.

At the end of each day after the children had said their prayers and she had extinguished the candles, Emily sat in the middle of her mattress holding a small tin box in her lap. Every night she opened the lid, and in the darkness counted its contents: a tarnished brooch, a faded likeness of her father, five copper pennies. She let her fingers linger over the pennies, wishing she could turn them into silver dollars.

That night as Emily slid the top back onto the box and slipped it under her blanket, she wished Mrs. Harmon weren't so demanding. Or that Lizzie were older and able to do more of the household chores without supervision. That would give Emily more time to run errands for Mr. Belden, or empty ore buckets at the Silver King Mine. Strong, Emily could do any task they might give her. She wouldn't mind walking six miles every day if she knew at the end of the week she would have another dollar to add to her savings. At one dollar a week, Emily calculated, in less than two months she would have enough money to leave Saw Tooth City. If she ate sparingly and did odd jobs along the way, she might even have enough money to take her as far as the Mississippi River with its majestic steamboats. But she would never be allowed to work at the Silver King Mine. Women near mines brought only misfortune. It would be just her luck that the very day she reported to work, the mine tunnel would collapse or the lumber in the stamp mill would catch fire.

If anyone asked Emily why she was so taken with the Mississippi, she wouldn't be able to say. She didn't even know herself. Perhaps it had something to do with the restless way the wind blew. Or the songs the robins sang, anticipating spring. More likely, it had something to do with Belden's handbill and the fact that she would soon turn sixteen. Sixteen was old enough to be married and free of her duties to the Harmons, but marriage was the last thing Emily wanted, to be tied to a man and a house full of hungry mouths to feed. Even though her servitude to the Harmons was grueling, she could still crawl into her own bed at night without worrying about meeting her husband's expectations. She'd heard the women talk when they thought she wasn't listening. She knew there were worse things than cooking and cleaning.

Emily lay back against her pillow. If she got up an hour earlier every day...if she didn't spend so much time looking at magazines when she should be working...Emily turned and faced the wall. It wouldn't matter. Even if she were to rise three hours earlier every day, Mrs. Harmon would only find more chores for her to do. She curled up under her blanket. Might as well face it. She'd have to find another way to earn some money, another way to leave Saw Tooth City. Until then, she would turn her attention to happier thoughts, to anticipating the arrival of the performing troupe and the famous Jenny Starr. She checked under her mattress for her worn handbill, content to know it was still there. Then she closed her eyes and let her imagination coax her to sleep.

The next morning Emily was more melancholy than usual, having concluded Saw Tooth City wasn't big enough after all to attract a famous troupe like Kerry Chapman's. Why else were they so late in arriving? Compared to Idaho City or Ketchum, Saw Tooth City must have seemed hardly worth the effort, a mere speck on a map of the frontier territory.

To chase away her disappointment, Emily busied herself with chores—dusting, sweeping floors, and hauling water up from Beaver Creek—until her arms and shoulders ached. Her afternoon passed routinely, and before long evening closed in, another uneventful day passing.

When the dishes were washed and put away, Emily joined the family in the parlor, where a kerosene lamp flickered on a table. Mrs. Harmon, busy with her needlework, didn't look up when Emily entered the room. Mr. Harmon, head bent over his daily ledgers, merely watched with narrowed eyes as Emily picked up her book and called to George and Lizzie. When the children were snuggled around Emily near the fireplace, Emily read by the wavering light.

"What!" said the master at length, in a faint voice.
"Please, sir," replied Oliver, "I want some more."
The master aimed a blow at Oliver's head with the ladle;
pinioned him in his arms; and shrieked aloud for the beadle.

"Really, Emily. Can't you find something more fitting? All this nonsense about shrieking and beatings is sure to give George and Lizzie nightmares." Her mood dour, Mrs. Harmon looked up from her stitches and glowered at Emily and her book.

Emily wanted to protest, to inform Mrs. Harmon that Charles Dickens was extremely entertaining, immensely popular as an author. She even had to pay Abe Pierson's son, Bobby, three cents just to borrow the book so she could read it to the children. But before Emily could open her mouth, the whinny of horses and the flash of lanterns drew their attention to the street.

Lizzie ran to the window and pushed aside the heavy curtain. "They're here!"

Mrs. Harmon stood and glanced at the oval mirror near the fireplace. She tucked a wandering lock of hair back in place, fixed a smile on her usually pinched face, and joined her husband, who had stepped forward and opened the door. "Welcome to Saw Tooth City," he said.

Emily watched as two men, clothes covered in the fine gray dust that seemed to coat everything in Saw Tooth City, assist a slim woman to the settee in front of the fire. A slightly older woman with hair the color of polished copper followed them into the room. These sorry-looking travelers couldn't possibly be their long-awaited thespians, Emily thought as she joined Lizzie at the window. Together they peered into the darkness, hoping for more promising arrivals. But there was nothing else to see, just a man standing outside near the horses.

Emily's mouth was dry. She tried to swallow. If disappointment had a flavor, it would taste like bitters, because that's what filled her mouth, tempting her to the kitchen for a glass of water. Before she could move, the door squeaked open and she turned as a tall man with a neatly trimmed goatee entered the room. He extended a white-gloved hand to Mr. Harmon. "Kerry Chapman," he said with a slight bow, "at your service." It was a good thing it was early spring and the mosquitoes and flies hadn't yet hatched, because Emily's mouth had dropped open so wide she would have swallowed a dozen of them with each uneven breath.

"Happy to make your acquaintance." Mr. Harmon accepted the offered hand and motioned to his spouse. "My wife, Mrs. Harmon."

"A pleasure to meet you, ma'am." Chapman removed his hat and bowed. He cradled Mrs. Harmon's hand in his own, bringing it theatrically to his lips. Emily's book thudded to the floor. She was staring, but she couldn't help it. Even covered in dust, Kerry Chapman was the most handsome man she had ever seen, counting the ones in Mrs. Harmon's magazines. His hair was so blond it was almost white, even in the darkest shadows of the parlor. Her breath caught as if she were tightly laced into one of Mrs. Harmon's corsets.

Chapman placed his hat and gloves on a side table and turned to the room like he would an audience. "Have you met the rest of my troupe?" He nodded to each as he introduced them. "Mr. Brooks, Mr. Ellerton, Miss Lewis, and Miss Starr." They, in turn, bowed like the accomplished actors they were, all except Miss Starr, who coughed into her handkerchief and winced when she shifted her leg. Mr. Brooks wasn't very tall, not much taller than Emily, and he reminded her of a penguin. Mr. Ellerton, on the other hand, stood heads above the others, clearly the tallest man in the room, and thinner than a slice of cheese.

None of them held her attention, though, like the woman seated near the fire. Emily was tempted to pull Belden's handbill from her pocket and compare the likeness. Surely this insignificant figure wasn't the Jenny Starr. She was too plain, too gaunt. Her hair was chopped short, like a man's, and it didn't shine like in the picture. In fact, it was quite dull-looking, as though it hadn't been washed in weeks.

"My, this is a fine establishment," Mr. Chapman said. "The finest I have seen in Idaho Territory."

His praise flustered Mrs. Harmon, who struggled to speak. "It's ah, ah—" When she finally composed herself, she blurted out, "Emily, go, bring these weary travelers something to eat."

Emily stared at the guests, groping for the book she'd dropped on the floor. When she rose, she stood face to face with Kerry Chapman himself.

"Emily," he smiled. "Such a charming name."

Even though there were several inches of air between them, Emily felt dizzy, like someone had forced every atom of oxygen from the room. She could feel his eyes on her shoulders, her bosom, but she couldn't turn away.

"Emily!"

She jumped at Mrs. Harmon's reprimand and hurried into the kitchen, where she readied a tray of sweet breads and coffee. When she returned with refreshments, Miss Lewis was chattering. "It was frightful. The axle broke and the wagon rolled, throwing us from the wagon. Thankfully, no one was killed. But look at our poor Jenny. She's lucky she didn't break a leg."

Miss Starr winced. "It was only sprained," she said, in a voice that did not sound as mellifluous as Emily had imagined.

Miss Lewis continued. "We were fortunate to run into Dr. Riley on his way to Vienna. He was kind enough to check our dear Jenny's leg. But the whole ordeal was terribly wearing." Miss Lewis brought her hand dramatically to her chest. As Emily offered the refreshments, she wondered if they even made corsets that big. Or if the corpulent woman had bathed recently.

"Thank you." Miss Lewis set her cup on the mantel. "I don't suppose you have any whiskey?" She rubbed her hands before the fire. "It gets bloody cold here once the sun goes down, doesn't it? How in the hell do ya stand it?"

Mrs. Harmon's head snapped back at Miss Lewis's crude language. Emily knew men talked that way in the mining camp, but she was sure Mrs. Harmon expected something better from the members of the troupe. "Ah—a few months from now we'll be complaining of heat and horseflies." Mrs. Harmon forced a laugh, and Emily was embarrassed by the way she chortled, sounding like one of Mr. Bidwell's pigs.

"It certainly is primitive," Miss Starr said from the settee. She took a sip of her coffee and gagged. "I thought I asked for tea."

Emily's faced burned even though she stood far away from the fire. Tea was a rare luxury in Saw Tooth City. She felt Mrs. Harmon's reprimand before she heard it. "Emily! Bring our guests some tea!"

Back in the kitchen, Emily shook the small tin, almost empty. While the water boiled on the stove, she wondered what to do. She didn't dare add coffee or dried chicory, which would make the brew too strong. She searched through the cupboards and located a jar of dried mint leaves and another of elderberry blossoms, which she spooned into the meager amount of tea, hoping it would do. Taking the tea into the parlor, Emily prayed the actress wouldn't ask for honey or milk. She was grateful when Miss Starr didn't request either.

"This certainly is an unusual blend," Miss Starr said as she sipped the drink and grimaced. She surveyed the room without interest and coughed into her handkerchief.

Emily glanced around the room, trying to see it through Miss Starr's eyes. Newly constructed, the building was less than a year old. The window drapings had been mail-ordered special from Chicago; the oak hall tree had arrived a few weeks ago. Just last fall she had helped Mrs. Harmon hang the wallpaper that now looked tacky and cheap, not much better than the magazine pages papering Mrs. Bidwell's kitchen. Harmon's Boarding House had the reputation of being the finest edifice in Saw Tooth City. And yet the diminutive woman sitting near the fire made Emily see clearly what she was just beginning to suspect. Saw Tooth City was just another dirty mining camp with nothing to impress fine visitors from the East. Not even a proper doctor. Not even a decent cup of tea. Ashamed, Emily retreated into a corner, wanting to disappear, to shrink smaller than a gnat stuck in the carpet.

"If you don't mind." Miss Starr's hand shook as she set her cup down. "I'd like to retire."

"Of course." Mr. Harmon motioned to the stairs. "Your rooms are ready. Please, follow me."

"Good night, Jenny dear," Mr. Chapman said as the two gentlemen set down their cups and stood out of respect. Their clothes were overlaid with dust, even after they'd sat and rested for a spell. Their hair too, looked like it could stand a good cleaning. But their manners were nothing less than eloquent as they assisted Jenny Starr to her room.

Running up and down the stairs fetching clean towels and fresh water for the guests, Emily wondered what it would be like to have two fine men like Brooks and Ellerton escort her to her room, or to own a fashionable dress like Miss Starr's, even if it was covered in dust. What she would really like was to hear Mr. Chapman say, "Good night, Emily dear." She laughed at her foolishness, pushing away the spell the troupe had begun to weave. But that didn't stop her from wishing it were true.

An hour later, with the house quiet and the new boarders settled for the night, Emily fidgeted with her prayers. Before she blew out the candle, she studied her handbill once more, carefully scrutinizing the picture of the pretty woman. Crawling into bed, she knew she wouldn't sleep. Not one wink. Not until she learned more about this strange assembly of people and what they had done with the real Jenny Starr.

CHAPTER THREE

"My life is one demd horrid grind!"
NICHOLAS NICKLEBY

EMILY YAWNED AS SHE scrubbed eggs and bacon grease from the black iron skillet. In less than two hours she would be back at the stove, preparing the noon meal. With a wet hand, she brushed a droopy lock from her face. She examined her hands, ashamed at the way the skin on her fingers puckered. They looked nothing like Miss Starr's slender fingers, or Miss Lewis's stubby ones—though she noticed Miss Lewis had a couple of broken fingernails, probably from their terrible accident, she concluded.

Emily rubbed a thumb over the calluses in her palm. One day she would have pretty hands, hands like Miss Starr's that never lifted a finger except to tie a ribbon. But for now, she plunged them back into the soapy water.

As she worked, her thoughts wandered to Belden's poster and the Mississippi River. In spite of the warm room and the perspiration running down her face, dragging her limp hair with it, Emily shivered. If the real Jenny Starr wasn't the same as the one on the poster, maybe the real Mississippi River wasn't as big as the one in the atlas. Maybe there were no steamboats. Maybe it was all make-believe, like the white rabbit in *Alice in Wonderland*. She searched the murky dishwater, speculating. Maybe the river was only as wide as Beaver Creek and even muddier. Or maybe there wasn't a Mississippi River at all.

Emily raised her hand, flinging water through the air. "Rubbish." Of course the river was there, right in Mr. Harmon's atlas. She'd traced it countless times with her finger.

Encouraged, she dried her hands, grabbed a broom and her housemaid's box, and headed for the stairs, thinking, if the river was real, then Jenny Starr was real, too. Maybe the picture on the handbill was taken a long time ago, when Miss Starr was feeling better.

She swept the stairs, paying close attention to any noise that might come from the corner bedroom. She assumed Miss Starr was still asleep since she hadn't joined the others for breakfast. Finished with the stairs and hallway, Emily lingered outside Miss Starr's door, seeking a reason to knock. Unable to find a suitable excuse to interrupt the woman's solitude, Emily turned away.

"Confound it all to hell!"

Emily almost dropped her broom at the profane words she heard coming from Miss Starr's bedroom. She jumped when she heard a crash and the sound of glass breaking.

As if responding to one of Lizzie's many mishaps, Emily pushed open the bedroom door without knocking. Inside the room, Miss Starr was struggling to regain her balance. Despite the doctor's tight wrap of arnica, Miss Starr's ankle was swollen, almost twice its normal size. The white ceramic ewer lay in pieces on the floor.

"Here, let me help." Emily eased the slight woman back into bed, tucking the pillows around her and making sure her foot was properly elevated.

"Thank you. I was just so thirsty."

Seeing the empty glass on the table and the puddle on the floor with the broken vessel, Emily said, "As soon as I get this cleaned up, I'll bring you fresh water. Would you care for anything to eat?"

"No," Miss Starr said. "I'm not hungry." She shifted on the bed and grimaced. "But I could use a sip of laudanum if you have any in the house."

"I'm not sure, but I'll see. I think we have some brandy, would that work?" Emily collected the broken bits of pottery and mopped the floor clean, then started to leave. "Are you sure you don't want any breakfast? You didn't eat a thing last night. You must be hungry."

Miss Starr waved her hand as if trying to wave away the discomfort in her leg. "Just something to ease the pain."

Emily hurried to the kitchen, where she disposed of her cleaning items and the broken mess. In the pantry she found a large Mason jar, which she filled with fresh water. She searched the shelves for the laudanum and was ready to give up when she spied the small brown bottle high on the top shelf. Fetching a stool, she reached for the bottle, disappointed to find that there was less than a tablespoon left. It would have to do. That and the brandy. Emily slipped the laudanum into her apron pocket along with a spoon and returned to Miss Starr's bedroom.

She tapped and without waiting for an answer pushed the door open. Miss Starr was lying on the bed, eyes closed, and at first didn't appear to hear Emily enter. It was only after Emily had settled the water, brandy, and bottle of laudanum on the table that Miss Starr stirred.

By this time Emily had had a chance to study Miss Starr's face and to compare it to the picture she carried in her pocket. She noticed the woman still wore the locket, even with her nightdress. That proved it, Emily concluded. The locket was the same as the one in the picture, she had no doubt.

Satisfied the figure lying in the bed was who she said she was, Emily said, "I have your medicine, Miss Starr."

The woman in the bed opened her eyes. "Thank you—," she whispered, trying to sit up. Assuming Miss Starr was reaching for a name, Emily provided one. "Emily. Emily McIntyre."

"Emily. Thank you, Emily McIntyre. Can you help me here? This damn foot is proving to be a nuisance." Miss Starr reached for the glass. Thinking she wanted water, Emily began to fill it.

"No," Miss Starr said. "Just the brandy and laudanum. For now, please."

Emily emptied the water into the washbasin and filled the glass with alcohol until Miss Starr nodded. "Now add the laudanum and mix it well."

Emily added the contents of the brown bottle, mixed the concoction, and gave it to Miss Starr. The woman drained the glass, and soon the wrinkles in her face relaxed and her hands stopped shaking. A smile played at the corners of her mouth, and she was almost as pretty as her picture. Emily was astonished at the transformation.

In the silence that filled the room, Emily fidgeted. She knew she should leave. She reached into her pocket, hesitated, but then pulled out the handbill. Not quite sure, she showed it to Miss Starr. "I—I can't tell you how much we've anticipated your arrival."

Miss Starr tilted her head and ran her hand through her short hair. That's when it occurred to Emily. The hair. Jenny Starr must have been wearing a wig in the picture. Odd how simply changing the length of one's hair changed one's appearance. Feeling happier than she had for days, Emily said, "I'm looking forward to hearing you sing."

"Thank you." The woman handed Emily the empty glass. "Whatever keeps a young thing like you in these primitive mountains? Is your husband a miner?"

Emily laughed. "I'm not married."

"You're not? You must be at least eighteen."

"Not quite." Emily stood taller. "Fifteen. Sixteen this fall."

"Why, at sixteen I was married and . . ." Miss Starr's voice faltered. "That was rude of me. It's none of my business." She shifted her weight and her pillow fell to the floor.

"Here, let me get that for you, Miss Starr."

"Jenny. Call me Jenny. Thank you." The pain had left the woman's face, and her disposition was decidedly brighter.

"That's a lovely locket," Emily said, tucking the pillow back in place.

"Thank you. It was a gift from my mother, just before she died."

"Oh, I'm sorry."

"Don't be," the singer said. "It was a long time ago."

Now that Emily was sure she was speaking with the very real Miss Jenny Starr, her tongue was tied. Should she comment on the weather? The accommodations? The troupe? She adjusted the pillow and asked, "This husband of yours, does he mind so much that you travel?"

Jenny started coughing, so hard the bed shook. Emily was ready to run for help when, trying to catch her breath and wiping tears from her eyes, Jenny broke into laughter. The laughter was so contagious, Emily joined her, and the pair laughed until they were exhausted and their faces were streaked with tears. They laughed like sisters; they laughed just to be laughing.

Jenny blew her nose. "I like you, Emily McIntyre. So, tell me. If you've no husband, what keeps you in this awful place?"

Emily looked at her hands.

If Jenny noticed Emily's discomfort, she didn't show it. "Let's see. McIntyre, isn't that Irish?"

Emily nodded. "Pa was born in Ireland."

"I see. Then it's safe to assume Mr. Harmon is not your father."

"My father's partner. Pa died some years ago."

"I'm sorry."

Emily swiped away a sudden tear and smiled. "The Harmons took me in when Pa died. I've been living with them since I was four."

"Four?" Jenny touched her locket, distracted for a moment before returning her attention to Emily. "So, tell me Emily, do you like Saw Tooth City?"

"It's not so bad. We moved here last summer from Rocky Bar. Just before they finished the sawmill. Mr. Harmon thought it would be good business."

"I see." Jenny lay back against her pillow, her face drawn, almost yellow compared to the linen pillowcase. "We're going to Rocky Bar. Is it as desolate as this place?"

Emily shook her head. "Oh, it's much bigger. There are more people. Although more and more are leaving, like we did." Then she added, "But I think you'll like it. I always did."

"So, Emily McIntyre, what did you like about Rocky Bar? Besides the miners and their money?"

Even though she resented Jenny's implications, Emily smiled, drawn to the brightness in Jenny's eyes when she teased. "It felt like home. My pa's buried there."

"And where's your mother?"

Emily looked at her fingers, her chipped nails, and mumbled. "Dead." It was a lie she repeated whenever she was asked about her mother. No matter how awful that might be, it was better than the truth.

There was a long silence as Jenny seemed to be remembering something. "I'm sorry," she said softly. "Would you be a love and run along now? I'd like to rest."

"Of course." She would have liked to visit more with Jenny, to stay longer and enjoy her newfound friend, and learn more about Jenny's husband or the East. But everyone was entitled to their privacy. So before the uneasiness that silence could bring to fill a room settled in, Emily left quietly and returned to her chores.

Later that day, sweeping dust from the front porch, Emily watched the troupe march down Main Street to promote their arrival. The handsome Mr. Chapman, leading the parade, looked annoyed. Emily watched him wave at the crowd, but his eyes did not smile. They were black and glinted like obsidian. Behind him, Miss Lewis and Mr. Ellerton danced as they sang selections from their repertoire. Mr. Brooks marched beside them, strumming lightheartedly on his banjo. Everyone was there but Jenny. Emily scanned the road for some sign of the singer. One by one, onlookers fell in step behind the troupe and soon Emily, too, was caught up in the excitement. She set the broom aside. Her feet followed as the group weaved through town toward the new community hall.

When Emily reached the building, she took a step back to watch. Mr. Chapman had taken off his black top hat and stood near the door with his hand extended. He held his hat upside down as he solicited twenty-five cents from adults and fifteen cents from children, all the while grinning like a jester. When he extended his hat to her, Emily stepped aside and plunged her hands into her empty pockets. She shouldn't have come. She had no business being there, but her feet wouldn't move. When Mr. Chapman had collected from all the paying customers, he reached into his pocket and withdrew some coins, which he slipped into Emily's hand. "Can't have a beauty like you miss my show, now can I?" He smiled at her and she all but stopped breathing.

The coins felt warm, almost hot, and Emily quickly dropped them into his hat, keenly aware of the way his cologne water filled the air around them, enticing and not at all like Mr. Harmon's obnoxious bay rum. He bowed and with his arm motioned her inside. Dazed by his presence, Emily fumbled her way to the end of a new hand-hewn bench and sat down.

After securing the revenue, Chapman took his place in the center of the stage. "Ladies and Gentlemen." He held his hands high. "It is with great pleasure that I bring to you the Kerry Chapman Troupe." The crowd applauded so hard the new windows rattled in their casings.

While the audience cheered, one by one the members of the company joined Chapman on stage. Miss Lewis paraded out singing, "Oh, don't you love an adventure?" Her voice was slightly off key; her large bosom protruded from her tight satin dress as she projected the lyrics. Brooks joined her in a duet and later captivated the crowd with a Shakespearean soliloquy. A skit in which Chapman was dashing as the Artful Dodger followed. After a brief intermission a curtain rose, and there, smiling brightly at the crowd from a velvet settee, was Miss Starr.

When Emily saw Jenny, she stood and clapped so hard her hands burned red. The rest of the audience stood and the sound of thunder inside the building increased until it seemed even the nails in the floorboards vibrated.

Emily thought that Jenny, her swollen ankle hidden under her long skirt, was prettier than her picture in the handbills scattered from St. Louis to Sacramento. The audience was so bewitched they didn't even notice when her voice broke on a high note. They didn't even notice she had to clear her throat often, or that between songs she sucked on lemons.

"When you go, you take my heart with you," Jenny began. Glancing around the room, Emily saw many red eyes. By the time Miss Starr finished her song, the room was so quiet Emily was sure men could hear their pocket watches tick, women could hear their babies sigh as they slept in their cribs back home.

"Brava, brava!" Applause filled the building.

"Thank you. Thank you for coming." Mr. Chapman led the troupe as they bowed to the crowd. Jenny, still on the velvet settee, waved her hand and blew kisses to the audience.

Later, Emily watched Chapman vigorously shake the hands of townsmen as they congratulated him on an afternoon of fine entertainment.

"That was a most delightful way to spend an afternoon." Mrs. Harmon pumped Chapman's hand. "I can't thank you enough for the complimentary tickets."

Emily couldn't help but notice the way Mrs. Harmon hovered, waiting until Mr. Chapman finally offered his arm. You would think he was Samuel Pickwick with a head full of blond hair, the way Mrs. Harmon made over him. Together, they walked down the dusty road to the boarding house, Mrs. Harmon praising the performers, Mr. Chapman smiling and nodding. When they passed Emily, he didn't even look her way.

But Emily noticed him, had watched him all afternoon with the exception of the few minutes she turned her eyes toward Jenny. How was it, she wondered, touching the place in her hand where he had dropped his coins, that just one look could make a heart burn like a fire that would never abate?

Mr. Chapman stood in the center of the parlor, and even though he was surrounded by cigar smoke and too many people, Emily suspected he had been watching her for some time too. His glance fell on her again, catching her staring at him, and she blushed. Her hands trembled, and she turned toward the kitchen.

"Emily," he called out, and the tray of empty glasses she carried shook, almost tipping a tumbler. He gently took the tray from her, set it on the kitchen table, and reached for her hand. "Kerry Chapman," he whispered, "at your service."

Too stunned to pull away, she shivered. He brought her fingers to his lips and kissed them until she felt they must be hot as coals. "So tell me, my good Emily, did you enjoy our show?"

"Yes, sir." The words stuck to the roof of her mouth like week-old oatmeal.

He towered over her and tilted his head intimately. "Do you think that I did justice to Charles Dickens?"

"I've seen none better," she said, casting her eyes at the floor.

"That is a most kind compliment." He grinned and leaned in closer. With his finger he lifted her chin until their eyes met. "I must tell you, I had the extreme pleasure of the great author's company in Washington during his second tour of America. Why, the man was brilliant, and he greatly inspired me. Remarkable, the way people flocked to his readings."

"You knew Charles Dickens?" He had her full attention, even though he'd ignored her earlier after the performance, even though he'd almost broken her heart with his indifference. He didn't have to ask; she had already forgiven him.

He placed a hand over his heart. "I was most fortunate. A young lad at the time, but equally impressed by his graciousness." He leaned forward so no one else could hear. "One evening after a reading, he tolerated a very poor performance I was coaxed into giving. He was kind and offered suggestions for improving my presentation. I have been most fortunate to consider him my mentor."

With admiration written across her face like a prayer, Emily said, "You were indeed, sir, most fortunate."

"Please, my good Emily. 'Sir' makes me sound old. Like my father." His laugh was hardy, and she blushed at his teasing.

"Not at all, sir. I mean Mr. Chapman. You hardly look like your father."

"Oh, ho. So you know my father, do you?" He gave her an exaggerated wink and smiled into her eyes, her heart. "Tell me, fair maiden, which do you prefer, the father or the son?"

Emily raised her hand to her mouth to suppress a giggle, but he stopped her by cupping her hand to his heart. "You must never hide your pretty face from me. You are lovely when you smile."

She blushed and he glanced toward the noise in the parlor. "I should get back to my friends before I am missed. But before I go, you must promise me a stroll sometime soon."

"It would be my pleasure," she said with a curtsey, something she had never done before except playing make-believe with George and Lizzie.

"No, my good Emily. The pleasure would be *mine*." With another kiss to her fingers, he returned to his admirers. Emily followed in a daze. He lit another cigar and blew a leisurely puff of blue smoke into the air, then pulled his watch from his pocket and stroked its gold chain. He grinned, and Emily believed she had never met anyone more alluring. And probably never would again.

Later, Emily lay on the small straw mattress and held her fingers to her lips. Suppressing a giggle, she remembered how it felt to have Kerry Chapman touch her, have him press his mouth against her fingers. Her breath caught, and her heart stopped for a minute as she remembered. She pulled the worn blanket over her head and laughed into her pillow. Her heart had never felt so giddy, her head so befuddled. Me. *Me*. He wants to go for a stroll with me.

If she'd been Lizzie, she would have clapped her hands, but the house was silent and the children slept just feet away, so she buried her head deeper into her pillow to muffle her happiness. As the minutes ticked toward morning, she imagined what he might say the next time they met. Already she could hear him: "How pretty you look, my good Emily."

She practiced an answer. "You are most kind, sir."

"Please, call me Kerry."

"You are most kind, Kerry." She closed her eyes and relished the way his name rolled from her lips, so sweet she could almost taste it. She fell asleep with the certainty that like a summer promise, he would fulfill all her dreams.

CHAPTER FOUR

The education of Mr. Jonas had been conducted from his cradle on the strictest principles...The very first word he learnt to spell was "gain," and the second (when he got into two syllables), "money."
MARTIN CHUZZLEWIT

THE NEXT MORNING EMILY pulled biscuits from the oven and set them on the counter to cool. The stove had finally driven the chill from the kitchen, and she slipped off her sweater.

"Smells delicious, Emily. You're going to make someone a good wife," Mrs. Harmon said from the doorway.

"Thank you," Emily said as she measured flour, milk, and eggs into a bowl. She beat the batter as though she were beating a rug. The last thing she wanted to be was someone's good wife. An accomplished seamstress with her own shop, maybe. Or, perhaps a clerk for Mr. Belden. Or—she barely dared to wish it—perhaps a professional singer like Jenny Starr. But never a good wife. *I've had enough cooking and cleaning to last a lifetime,* she thought—until she heard Mrs. Harmon say his name.

"I was surprised to see you at the Kerry Chapman performance yesterday. Where did you get the money to attend?"

Emily had already anticipated the question and answered. "I've—I've been able to earn a little by doing odd jobs for Mr. Belden." Not really a lie, though not the truth either.

"When do you have time?" Mrs. Harmon tapped her finger against the counter as if counting her years as Emily's guardian. When Emily didn't answer, Mrs. Harmon frowned, dropped her half-eaten biscuit into the slop bucket, and left the room.

Relieved she didn't have to disclose the truth, or give a detailed account of the errands she had performed for Mr. Belden, Emily's thoughts wandered to the coins, to the show, and Kerry Chapman. The mere suggestion of his name made her heart ache, and she lost herself deep in a daydream.

"Emily?"

She jumped, spilling batter down the front of her dress and onto the floor. She looked up to find Miss Lewis standing in the doorway holding a pink garment.

"I've interrupted your thoughts," Miss Lewis said. "And from the look on your face, they must have been very pleasant."

Emily's face burned. She felt like she had suddenly sprouted thirteen arms, each with a mind of its own, because instead of leaning down and mopping up the floor, she was smearing the batter around in circles.

"I'm sorry I startled you. I was hoping you could point me to a dressmaker to fix my costume."

"Mostly only miners here right now," Emily mumbled. Finished with the floor, she wiped her hands on her apron. "Let me see it." She examined the soft material, turning the dress inside out. She gently pulled the fabric to see if it would still unravel. "How soon do you need it fixed?"

"Before evening?"

"That soon," Emily said. By now the first batch of hotcakes was burning, not fit to eat. She would have to throw them out and start all over.

She removed the skillet from the stove, left the room, and returned with her sewing basket. She settled into a chair, and in less than ten minutes she had reseamed the dress and fixed the ravels.

"You're a gem," Miss Lewis said, slipping a coin into Emily's pocket. Before she left, she whispered. "Don't let Mr. Chapman know you're so talented with a needle, or he'll steal you away from the Harmons. We haven't had access to a proper seamstress in ages."

When Miss Lewis was gone, Emily reached into her pocket and examined the coin, a silver dollar. She felt a little dizzy from its weight, more money than she had had, ever. She wrapped it in a tissue and tucked it back into her pocket. While she stoked the stove and began a new batch of hotcakes, her thoughts returned to Miss Lewis's warning. Mr. Chapman steal her away? Not likely. Nonetheless, the mere notion made her lightheaded. A smile teased the corner of her mouth, a giddiness fluttered her heart. The flutter was caused by more than just the thought of mending his costumes. A longing came from a place deep inside her, from a place she never even knew existed. Her pulse quickened as she flipped the pancakes, practicing to make them perfect, the way a husband would expect. *For you, my darling.* She practiced balancing the plate and tipping her neck for a husband's appreciative kiss.

Now Emily had two wishes. If she had to pick between Mississippi steamboats and Kerry Chapman, she would have a hard time choosing. Settling the fresh hotcakes on the platter, she remembered the way her breath caught when he pressed the coins into her hand, the way his cologne water made her want more than his kind words. Smiling, she had an answer. She knew without a doubt which one she'd choose.

CHAPTER FIVE

In another moment down went Alice after it, never once considering how in the world she was to get out again.
Lewis Carroll, ALICE IN WONDERLAND

THE KERRY CHAPMAN TROUPE had been in Saw Tooth City less than a week and already the chokecherries were starting to bloom. Emily had been so busy she hadn't noticed winter had packed its bags and finally left the valley, not until after she dipped her bucket into the swollen waters of Beaver Creek and inhaled the fragrant breeze of the silver pine and muddy soil. She set down her sloshing, overfilled pails and stopped to gather a handful of white blossoms, planning to surprise Jenny with the sweet bouquet. The actress had been so irritable Emily hoped the smell of spring would lift her spirits.

Thinking of Jenny, Emily frowned. She had hoped they would have more time to visit, more time to laugh. But the troupe too had been busy—away at the Silver King, Last Chance, and Columbia mines until hours late into the night—and Emily had scarcely seen Jenny, let alone Kerry Chapman. Even now they were off entertaining the workers near the Galena Mines.

After filling the water reservoir in the stove, Emily settled the buckets near the sink and fetched a pretty jar for the blossom sprigs. She set it above the sink, planning to take it to Jenny's room later. Opening the back door, she called outdoors to Lizzie, "Bring your book."

Since the boarding house was empty and Mrs. Harmon was napping, Emily and Lizzie snuggled into the settee in the parlor. "Chapter Five," Emily read aloud. "Advice from a Caterpillar."

Lizzie laughed when Emily puckered her mouth and read, pretending to blow smoke from a hookah, "Who are you?"

"Who are youuuuuuu?" Lizzie imitated Emily. They scrunched up their noses and laughed. A board creaked and they turned at the sound.

"You surprised us," Emily said to Jenny Starr, losing her place in the book. "I thought you were with the others over at the Pilgrim."

"I was too ill to go." Jenny's eyes were hollow and her hands shook, ever so slightly. A strange odor clung to her clothes, along with the heady smell of gardenias.

"Can you get these items for me?" Jenny gave Emily a list along with a purse of coins. "I would go, but I still don't get around very well on this damned, oh, excuse me—" She took notice of the child. "Sorry, sweetheart, I forget your name—this confounded foot of mine."

"Lizzie. This is Lizzie." Emily considered the list, remembering Mr. Belden's reproach from the day before. "Again?" he had asked when she requested the laudanum. Slipping the list into her pocket, Emily said, "Can I get you anything else while I'm there?"

"No, that should be sufficient."

Emily handed the book to Lizzie. "I shouldn't be long. Mark our place."

"Miss Starr," Lizzie said. "Would you like to read with me?"

"I…I—" Jenny stammered as though seeking an excuse.

"It's a very funny book. It will make you laugh."

"Lizzie," Emily said. "We mustn't bother Miss Starr. She isn't feeling well."

"I'll read to her," Lizzie responded. "It will make her feel better." Lizzie opened the book and prepared to read.

If fear had a color, Emily knew it must be white, because that was the color Jenny's face turned when Lizzie grabbed the singer's hand and pulled her to the bench.

"Lizzie," Emily scolded.

But Jenny said, "Go. We'll be fine." Even though she smiled, her almost inaudible, unsteady voice belied her words.

"We'll be fine," Lizzie parroted, and pointed to the door. "Go."

"Are you sure?"

"Yes," Jenny said. "Don't worry. It's been years since I did this. But I'm sure Lizzie here will help me with the big words." Jenny looked uncomfortable. Emily knew Lizzie could be a handful if she had a mind to. But seeing Lizzie's eager face as Jenny settled next to her, Emily relented. "I won't be long. I promise." Tying her bonnet, she added, "Lizzie, mind your manners while I'm gone."

Emily moved as quickly as her feet would carry her. She didn't stop to converse with Mr. Belden but hurried home, running the last few steps. When she opened the door, Lizzie was saying, "In the summer we have lots of eggs. It's my job to gather them. Every single day."

Jenny, as if in a daydream herself, smiled attentively and brushed a lock of hair away from Lizzie's eyes. But when she caught sight of Emily, she startled and moved away from Lizzie.

"Hope I wasn't gone too long." Emily handed a brown paper package to Jenny.

"We were just getting started," Lizzie said with a pout.

"Sorry." Emily smiled an apology to Jenny. "She loves books."

"You are a very lucky little girl, Lizzie, to have someone like Emily to read to you."

For a moment Emily thought she saw melancholy written in Jenny's face. Abruptly the image disappeared.

"Emily, thank you. I'm tired. I think I'll go to my room." When Jenny left the parlor, she left behind the smell of gardenias and something else. A sadness Emily had no name for unless it was loneliness, envy, and regret.

The next morning, Emily stood in the middle of the doorway, wordlessly clutching clean towels as she watched Jenny and Miss Lewis pack. Surely the troupe couldn't be moving on so soon, Emily thought. They folded their clothes and tucked them into the trunk while Emily watched, all the while wishing there was some way she could stop them, some way to detain them for one more day.

"Don't look so forlorn," Miss Lewis said. "It's not the end of the world."

But it felt that way to Emily. It felt as though her future had trickled between the cracks in the floorboards as she watched the women prepare to leave.

Jenny and Miss Lewis examined the room once more to make sure they hadn't forgotten something, then turned towards the door with their satchels. "Goodbye, Emily. Maybe we'll meet again some day," Jenny said.

Emily's throat was so dry she couldn't speak. She tried to smile when Miss Lewis said, "Thanks, kid, for everything."

"Safe trip." The words stuck to Emily's tongue. But before the women reached the stairs, Emily stammered. "Miss Lewis?"

The performer turned. Now that she had Miss Lewis's attention, Emily hesitated. Without meeting the trouper's gaze, Emily said, "I was wondering. I mean, do you think Mr. Chapman would consider hiring me?"

Miss Lewis placed a comforting hand on Emily's shoulder. "You're going to make someone a good wife, kid. Take care of yourself."

I don't want to make someone a good wife, Emily wanted to scream. Unless that man was Kerry Chapman. She pursed her lips into a half-smile, biting back her disappointment as the woman with hair the color of polished copper turned and followed Jenny Starr down the stairs.

Outside, most of the town had gathered around the departing troupe. Emily pushed her way forward and watched Jenny and Miss Lewis climb into the wagon. She wondered what would happen if she were to climb into the wagon beside them. The very notion made her dizzy.

As if her heart wasn't beating fast enough, she saw Mr. Chapman stroll toward her. She almost forgot to breathe.

"My good Emily. How very nice to see you again." He pulled her chapped hands into his and lowered his voice so only she could hear. "I'm sorry we didn't get to take that stroll, but I've word of a new strike near Vienna. We're on our way now but I promise you, we will return to Saw Tooth City and you and I shall have that walk. Till then, keep me in your heart and a smile upon your lovely face."

He brushed her fingers with his lips. Her heart pounded so hard she was sure he could hear it and she wondered why he couldn't see her desperation, her need to go with him, when he looked into her eyes.

"Now I must go." He bowed to the crowd. "Look for us soon. We shall return."

Emily watched until the wagon rounded the corner and disappeared behind the livery. Then she ran back inside the boarding house and up the stairs. She pushed open the bedroom door and rushed to the window. When she saw the members of the troupe waving farewell to the young children following the wagon down the dusty road, she whispered aloud the wish that had formed in her heart. "Please take me with you."

Please take me with you. Her whisper became a prayer, one she repeated over and over again as she ran down the stairs, through the kitchen and into her bedroom. She grabbed her tin box and sweater and ran out the back door as fast as her feet would go.

* * *

Emily was less than a mile out of town when she spotted something in the road ahead. She slowed her pace and squinted. Not a doe. Maybe a bear? She took deep breaths to slow her pulse and proceeded with caution. The object wasn't moving. She heard a horse whinny, and raced forward.

It was the wagon, tipped lopsided on the road, one of its wheels deep in a rut. A steamer trunk, lodged topsy-turvy beside a giant fir, was spilled open, scattering several muslin evening robes, a man's claw-hammer coat, bonnets with lace and partridge feathers, corsets, and black bowlers across the road and under the evergreens. "Oh, no," Emily cried and raced toward the wreckage, her blond hair flapping in the wind. *Where was everybody? Were they hurt?*

By the time Emily reached the hapless group, Mr. Chapman was brushing the dirt from his clothes. Miss Lewis was lamenting over the large rip in her dress, and Jenny sat at the side of the road, rubbing her ankle. Mr. Ellerton tried to calm the horses while Mr. Brooks began to collect the scattered items. Panting so hard she had to hold onto the back of the wagon, Emily bent over to catch her breath. Her heart thudded so fast she thought she'd expire. At least they were safe. She kept her head down until the dizziness passed, then hurried to help collect the costumes strewn along the muddy road like trinkets from a peddler's runaway cart. When Emily returned to the wagon, it was standing straight again and Mr. Chapman was helping Jenny into her seat. Emily squared her shoulders and with deliberate steps approached Mr. Chapman. She wiped the dirt from her sweaty cheeks and winced, knowing she must look worse than a common kitchen maid. Just the same, she lifted her chin. "If you have room for me, sir, I would like to come along," she said to him. She took another deep breath. "I can work hard. I can cook, sew. I don't eat much and I won't be a bother." Her words tumbled over each other. She prayed he wouldn't laugh at her confusion, and the words rolling from her mouth like marbles.

Chapman leaned forward and said, "There, there, my good Emily. You're welcome to go wherever we go. But won't your guardians be worried?"

"I'll write them as soon as I'm able," she said. "Besides, I'm old enough to take care of myself."

He hesitated only a moment before he said, "Well, then. How can I refuse?"

Emily jumped into the wagon before he could change his mind. She settled next to Jenny and asked, "Are you hurt?"

Jenny shook her head. "You don't want to do this."

"Oh, yes I do," Emily said adamantly. "I know exactly what I'm doing." She settled into the seat and avoided looking at the others. When Miss Lewis turned a raised eyebrow in her direction, Emily looked away.

"Shall we be off?" Chapman said, and Ellerton flicked the whip to move the horses.

So grateful she could practically fly, Emily folded her hands firmly in her lap and looked straight ahead while the wagon rolled down the road toward Vienna. She didn't look back toward Saw Tooth City. She didn't let herself dwell on how the Harmons, and especially Lizzie and George, might worry, either. She didn't let herself think about how hasty she had been or what she had left behind. She was even more afraid of what lay ahead, but she was determined not to show it. Instead, she watched Ellerton guide the horses past a fallen pine tree and through a patch of yellow mule's-ears, almost as attentively as she would watch a fortune teller unveil her future.

CHAPTER SIX

"Who in the world am I? Ah, that's the great puzzle!"
ALICE IN WONDERLAND

FOR A WHILE, THE ONLY sound in Saw Tooth Valley was the crunch of gravel as the wagon rolled over the dusty road. Emily was nauseous even though the rejuvenating smell of spring filled the air. She didn't know if the pip in her stomach was caused from running so hard, or from regret. Or, quite possibly, from another chance to be near Kerry Chapman.

Ellerton turned the wagon south through scrub timber and sagebrush. Emily glanced over her shoulder toward Saw Tooth City. She smiled, trying to mask the misgivings piling up inside her like dirty laundry. No one was talking, but she could feel the unasked questions riding along in the wagon as, one by one, the members of the troupe diverted their eyes away from her and toward the passing scenery. She was glad that the jostling wagon, wheels crunching and grinding over the crushed-granite road, made proper conversation impossible. Occasionally she tilted her head in Mr. Chapman's direction. His smile reassured her. Little by little she relaxed, confident she had made the right decision.

A few miles down the road Mr. Chapman leaned forward and said, "Why don't we teach Emily that little ditty we sang yesterday?"

Jenny and Miss Lewis exchanged knowing glances and indulged their manager. "The miners came in forty-nine . . ." they began in unison. Ellerton gave Brooks the reins, turned in his seat, faced the women, and blew into his harmonica while he tapped his feet against the wooden floor of the wagon.

Suddenly cold in spite of the sunshine, Emily couldn't move. She'd heard the song many times before. And she could never listen without feeling the words were directed at her—and her mother. "Goldie," they called her, even though her real name was Sarah. "Idaho Gold," the miners taunted, even in Saw Tooth City, unaware that the nickname made Emily feel used and dirty. "If you're ever near the mining camp of Atlanta, be sure to pay Goldie a visit."

"Come, Emily," Mr. Chapman said. "Do join us." He recited the first four lines and she wiped her hand across her brow, thankful she could blame the sun for her flushed face, wishing she had thought to grab her bonnet before she ran away. She felt a knot in her stomach and wondered if she had been hasty after all, that she may have been better off with the people she knew back in Saw Tooth City instead of this strange cast of characters.

But the troupe seemed friendly, happy to have her along. If they harbored any malice, it didn't show; they seemed lighthearted and jolly, even Miss Lewis. They continued singing, and the tune began to sound as familiar as one of the nursery rhymes she always sang to George and Lizzie. Even though the lyrics made her squirm, made her remember things she would rather forget, when Kerry Chapman looked at her and smiled, she forgot everything except how much she wanted to please him. Pushing down her embarrassment, she took a deep breath and sang along as they harmonized, "And when they got together / they produced the native son."

At first she choked on the word "whore," struggling to push away her revulsion. It was just a song, just a word. It had nothing to do with her. Or her mother. She tried again, this time closing her eyes and thinking of "chores" instead of the offending word, and soon the song rolled easily through her teeth.

"That was magnificent," Mr. Chapman said. "Quite suitable for your lovely voice. Now try this one."

They sang "Oh, Susanna" and "My Grandfather's Clock." By the time they reached Vienna, the mountaintops shone gold above the purple evening shadows and Emily realized there was nothing personal in their random choice of songs. They were just tunes. It hadn't tarnished her one bit to sing the off-color words along with this merry group, a group that made her feel welcome, as though she had finally found a home.

* * *

The smell of freshly cut timber lingered in the rapidly freezing night air. Emily could make out forty or fifty buildings, most of them new, scattered haphazardly up and down Front Street. Every bare piece of ground appeared to have something on it—a soon-to-be-completed structure, round or square canvas tents, plank shacks, log cabins. Even in the twilight it was clear to see that although Saw Tooth City was booming, Vienna was growing much faster.

In some ways it reminded her of Rocky Bar with all its hustle and bustle. She smiled at Mr. Chapman, grateful for a chance to visit a new place, to be a part of something more than washing dishes and tending children.

Brooks stopped the wagon in front of a large building bearing the words ABBOTT HOTEL on its fancy wooden facade. One by one the jostled troupe members stiffly stepped down, away from the wagon. Emily alighted and glanced about as if afraid to move. What would the troupe's arrangements be at a hotel? Would she need money? Should she offer to carry in the hand luggage? Miss Lewis and Jenny, who now walked unassisted but with a slight limp, had already entered the hotel. Mr. Chapman, busy with the business of notoriety, had once again forgotten her. Hoping to make herself useful, Emily picked up as many satchels as she could carry and stepped up onto the wooden sidewalk and into the inn.

Inside, she was stunned by what she saw. Her mouth dropped open as she faced a massive marble desk. Yards and yards of embossed blue brocade hung on the walls. The room was illuminated with fancy glass lamps. Emily dropped the luggage and stared at the tapestries, the chandeliers, and the floor that was covered with plush maroon carpet. She didn't know she was gawking until Jenny prompted from the stairway. "Emily, are you coming?"

Quickly, she followed Jenny up the stairs. In the room she learned she was to share with Jenny and Miss Lewis, Emily sat on the edge of an intricately carved chair and watched Jenny wash the dust from her face. When it was her turn, Emily timidly reused the dirty water in the bowl. She reached for a towel and hesitated. Should she use the one Jenny used or the clean towel hanging on the end of the washstand? Unable to decide, Emily pulled her handkerchief from her pocket and blotted her wet cheeks, leaving the clean towel for Miss Lewis. Running her fingers through her tangled hair, she longed for a comb and wished her dress wasn't so common.

Miss Lewis mentioned food, and Emily's stomach rumbled. She brushed at the mud clinging to the hem of her skirt and followed the women down the stairs, hoping the few coins she had would be enough to cover her meal and lodgings. It occurred to her to slip back to her room unnoticed and forego the expense of the evening meal, but she was hungry. So hungry her stomach ached. *I won't be poor forever*, she thought as she entered the dining room.

Oh. Every thought in her head vanished when Emily saw the elaborate chandelier reflected in the large mirrors covering each wall of the room. Everywhere she looked candles twinkled like a million tiny pieces of quartz crystals glittering in the noonday sun.

This was no Wonderland tea party, Emily thought as she slipped into the chair beside Jenny. Grander than anything she had ever seen in *Frank Leslie's Popular Monthly*, the table was set with fresh linen cloths, silver napkin rings, and pattern-glass finger bowls. She could smell the delicious aromas of the oyster soup, fresh bread, and baked salmon even before the meal was served.

"Pass the butter," Brooks said with a nod, rousing Emily from her reflections.

She passed the dish without helping herself first. When she bit into the bread, she didn't even notice—it was so moist it didn't need condiments. She chewed eagerly, her stomach grumbling for more. It was only after she had finished her soup and started in on the fish that she remembered. This was the first meal she had eaten in a long time that she didn't help prepare. She took a bite of the salmon and smiled. Every bite tasted better than desire.

Jenny and Miss Lewis barely touched their food, but Emily ate until she was full, until her belly could hold no more. Drowsy from the lavish feast, Emily shook her head to stay awake. She was relieved when Jenny announced, "It's time to retire."

Upstairs in their room wearing a beige sacque chemise borrowed from Jenny, Emily watched Miss Lewis—*Bella,* Emily had been instructed to call her—brush the dust from her long red hair. It was a pretty color, almost unnatural, and Emily wondered what Bella used to make it glisten. Vinegar? Ammonia?

She examined a strand of her own hair, dull blond in comparison. Maybe, when she had more money and knew them better, she would ask, "Just what is it you use on your hair to make it shine so?"

But not now. Right now she was even too tired for female conversation. She slipped under the covers and suppressed a giggle. A real mattress. It hardly mattered that she had to share the bed with Bella. She would rather it be Jenny, but she understood. The star needed her rest. She patted the bed and snuggled deeper under the covers. At least it wasn't a pile of straw on the floor.

As she closed her eyes to what felt like the longest day of her life, Emily considered her future. Tomorrow she must find work. She must also find a way to repay Mr. Chapman for his kindness and for rescuing her from Saw Tooth City.

Yawning, Emily considered her options. Perhaps she could sew for the troupe. Or, if they didn't need her services, maybe she could offer to work for Mr. Abbott. She wouldn't mind one bit working in an establishment as fine as this. She wouldn't even mind cleaning the chandeliers.

Or, Emily thought, if she brushed her hair every day it might shine brighter than Bella's. Maybe then Emily would be pleasing enough to win forever the heart of every man, even the heart of Kerry Chapman.

CHAPTER SEVEN

That was a memorable day to me, for it made great changes in me.
GREAT EXPECTATIONS

IT WAS LATE, long after breakfast, before Emily stirred. And it wasn't the thought of food that woke her; her stomach was still full from the night before. Rather, it was the noise outside her room, the sound of sweeping and the smell of furniture polish that coaxed her awake. She struggled to lift heavy eyelids, thinking she must get moving. Mrs. Harmon was sure to be vexed if she was doing Emily's chores. Or trying to make Lizzie do them. Emily opened her eyes and remembered. She was no longer in Saw Tooth City. She was in the big, bustling city of Vienna. But she was also alone. Bella's side of the bed was empty. Bella was nowhere in the room. Neither was Jenny.

Reluctant to leave the warm feather bed, Emily scolded herself into action. This would never do; they would think her lazy, sleeping half the day away. She slipped from the bed, making it up neatly before she dressed. She washed her hands and scrubbed her teeth with the end of a towel, wishing for her toothbrush. She looked longingly at Bella's hairbrush. Should she use it—would Bella care? No, Emily decided, probably not.

She picked up the brush and stroked her hair, imitating Bella's movements from the night before. If she brushed her hair every day, maybe she would be . . . Emily slapped the brush onto the dresser. Determined to make up for oversleeping and disgusted with herself for primping when she should be working, she twisted her hair into a knot and hurried from the room to find the troupe. She stopped short in the hall when she encountered the maid.

Upon seeing Emily, the small Chinese woman dropped her gaze to the floor and stepped back to let her pass.

"Good morning," Emily said uneasily. "It looks to be a pleasant day."

Without moving her gaze from the floor, the woman nodded. Emily felt guilty making her way down the stairs toward the parlor. Guilty, and yet a bit relieved. Guilty because she had run out on the Harmons without a word of good-bye. Relieved because she didn't have to sweep the stairs today, or dust the furniture either. She entered the parlor, where a young maid advised Emily that the troupe had departed; they weren't expected back until after nightfall.

"Can I get you something to eat?" the maid asked.

"No, thank you," Emily said. "You mustn't bother."

"No bother at all, Miss." The maid waited expectantly for Emily to dismiss her.

"That will be all." Emily felt very grown up giving orders to someone besides George and Lizzie. But also a bit giddy. Judging by appearances, she was younger than the parlor maid, and perhaps might soon be working there beside her.

"Yes, ma'am." The maid collected her broom and housemaid's box, leaving Emily to wander alone in the large room adorned with an entire matching suite of parlor furniture and a grand mahogany table. Emily stroked the dark red velvet chairs. Someday she would own something this nice. But for now, she must make herself useful. She must find a constructive way to use her time until the troupe returned.

Back upstairs, alone in the room she shared with Jenny and Bella, Emily glanced at the large trunk that contained their wardrobe. Unable to curb her curiosity, she knelt on the floor in front of the large leather chest and one by one took out the contents, mostly costumes. Some were dirty. Many were torn. The spill on the road out of Saw Tooth City had left some of them in less than stageworthy condition.

Deciding this would be a good way to show how handy she was with a needle, Emily searched the room for something with which to mend the clothes. Finding nothing, she returned to the trunk. If she couldn't mend them, she could at the very least brush and straighten them.

At the bottom of the trunk she found a small metal box containing spools of thread, buttons, pins, a pair of scissors, and a paper of needles. She dragged a chair next to the open chest, forced a strand of silk through the eye of a needle, and began to sew. Pulling thread through a yellow feather, Emily recognized the boa as the one Bella wore when she had performed back in Saw Tooth City. Emily reattached the feathers to the long scarf and imitated Bella, singing, "I can - not dance to - night . . ." Finished, Emily looped the boa around her neck, stood and twirled around the room to the make-believe sound of Brooks's banjo. "Thank you very much," she said breathlessly, bowing to her pretend audience. "It has been my great pleasure to perform for you tonight."

She carefully folded the boa and picked up a torn chemise. She sang while she mended item after item, sometimes pantomiming if she recognized a costume. She worked well into the afternoon, picking up a man's shirt that was missing a button. She held it to her nose and inhaled. Ugh. She pushed the offensive garment from her face. Definitely not Mr. Chapman's.

She replaced the button and reached into the trunk for another garment. She was troubled when she came across a red corset trimmed with black lace. The lace had been ripped from the bodice. Odd to have a delicate piece of clothing destroyed so brutally, as if someone had tried to tear it away rather than take the time to unlace it. With black thread, Emily carefully reattached the lace strips. When finished with her latest handiwork, she carried the corset to the mirror and held it up to her body. *Just about my size.* She turned in front of the mirror. Checking her reflection, she flinched; the corset was so revealing it was disgraceful, even for underwear. She shoved the black-laced garment under the pile of mended clothes. She would never wear something so daring. But not before she stroked the exotic lace one more time. Interrupted by a knock, Emily crossed the room and opened the door to the Chinese woman.

"We are serving dinner soon. Will you be joining us in dining room or would you like I bring up tray?"

"Oh, you needn't bother with a tray." Emily was flustered but quickly regained her composure before the little woman. "I'll come down. How long before dinner is served?"

"About thirty minutes, Missy." The woman turned and hobbled down the stairs, leaving Emily standing in the doorway.

Emily closed the door. What was she thinking? She couldn't go down to dinner alone—how would that look? Besides, she had nothing to wear. She brushed at the stains on her skirt. She would starve before she wore her soiled dress to dinner again. Distraught, she fell into the chair until her stomach complained, reminding her that she hadn't eaten lunch. Taking several deep breaths, she gathered her thoughts. There had to be something in that trunk that would fit her. She raised the lid and rummaged through the clothing: a man's shirt, a slip that looked like a nightgown. Near the bottom of the pile, her hands lingered over a red velvet gown. She pulled the dress out and held it in front of her, so different from anything she had ever worn before. The smell of food reminded Emily she didn't have a lot of time, so she slipped into the dress, the first real dress she had tried on that actually touched the floor.

Cocking her head to one side, she studied her reflection in the mirror. If only it had more material to cover her shoulders. Well, it didn't; it would have to do. She hesitated only a moment before fastening the buttons. Except for its length, it would serve without alterations.

With her hair pinned up and her shoulders bared, Emily was sure she must look older than fifteen. She blushed at her reflection, hardly recognizing herself, but pleased with what she saw. She tidied her hair and, after one last look in the mirror, descended the stairs to the dining room, trying to remember to keep her head high and her shoulders back, and to smile politely.

At the bottom of the stairs, Mr. Abbott greeted her. "Miss Emily, how nice to see you. I'm pleased you are joining us for dinner. Did you have a restful day?"

Emily faltered. *He's making fun of me.* She turned away but before she could retreat, another couple joined them in the hallway.

Trapped, she took a deep breath and said, "Yes, thank you." She followed Mr. Abbott into the dining room and slipped into the chair being held for her by Mr. Ross, another boarder, all the time trying to remember to smile. All the time hoping she wouldn't sound too common or appear as nervous as her shaking legs confirmed.

They were an intimate group gathered in the dining room. Mr. and Mrs. Wilson—newlyweds on the order of David and Dora Copperfield, Emily judged by the way they kept gazing into each other's eyes—sat to her right. An older gentleman, perhaps an attorney like Mr. Spenlow, sat to her left, and at the head of the table was a tall, thin man, a proprietor, judging by his fine dark suit. Overwhelmed, Emily wished for the comfort of the troupe, the pleasantries that had spilled around the dining-room table the night before.

The previous evening had been easy enough for Emily to manage. There was so much confusion she was all but forgotten. But tonight she was the only one at the table representative of the Kerry Chapman Troupe, and all eyes were on her as the other guests likely took her for one of the performers. With a deep breath she tried to live up to their expectations.

"Good evening," she said to her dinner companions. She smiled and settled her napkin quietly in her lap. Seeing the conservative way Mrs. Wilson was dressed, Emily wished her own red dress were less revealing. But it was too late for that. She must get through the meal without embarrassing herself or the troupe. Emily tried not to stare at the Chinese woman near the sideboard, who was ladling steaming soup into blue and white bowls decorated with oriental motifs and quickly setting the bowls in front of the diners.

"Excellent," Mr. Ross said upon trying the broth. "I do believe this is the best onion soup I have tasted since leaving Chicago."

Emily held her spoon tighter. They hadn't had onions all winter. She was hungry, eager to begin. Cautious, she waited and watched the others. She didn't move until Mrs. Wilson picked up her spoon and began to eat. Then, with a slight quiver, Emily dipped her own spoon into her bowl in a manner similar to that of her fellow diners and savored the soup's full flavor. Onion soup with real cream, one of her favorites.

Soon everyone at the table was eating, and slowly the uncomfortable silence filled with discussions of gold prices, the wet spring, and completion of the new Apollo Hall.

"So, Miss Emily," Mr. Ross said, "are you enjoying Vienna?"

Glad that she had just taken a big bite of roast duck, Emily nodded silently.

"Well, Vienna is certainly looking forward to your troupe's performance. We haven't had lively entertainment in these parts for some time." Mr. Ross tipped his wine glass and took a long drink. Emily followed her roast duck with a sip of lemonade and turned her attention to the green beans on her plate. When addressed, she answered as quickly and politely as possible, thankful no one asked personal questions or tried to make her feel out of place. Occasionally she caught the men staring at her, but they were quick to look away.

Even after dessert had been served and the boarders had retired to their rooms, the troupe had still not returned. Reluctant to remain alone in her chambers, Emily located a wool shawl and walked from the hotel onto the wooden boardwalk, inhaling the crisp night air. Dusk settled around her like a blanket as she strolled to the end of the block. She picked up her skirt to maneuver the wooden stairs, glad the dress was long enough to hide her ragged shoes.

She walked one block. And another. She walked quickly as she passed a building rumored to be a house of ill repute. She tried not to look through the window, wondering if her mother might be there behind that door instead of in a boarding house back in the rugged mining town of Atlanta.

Quickly diverting her thoughts, she hummed as she thought about her pleasant dinner company and her productive day. She was sure that when Mr. Chapman saw her fine mending he would be more than happy to offer her employment. Lost in her daydreams of Mr. Chapman, she was surprised to find that she had traveled farther than intended. She turned back toward her lodgings, and it wasn't long before she spotted the glow of the Abbott Hotel, where light and merriment spilled out into the street like a golden elixir. She hastened her step, curious to see what she was missing.

When she reached the hotel, the number of people gathered near the door amazed her. The sound of plinking piano keys filtered into the street, and her first thought was that Mr. Abbott played rather well. She lingered outside, inhaling the gaiety that floated with the music into the night air. When the music stopped, a whisper rippled through the crowd. Then the piano plinked again, and she heard Jenny's voice.

Emily stretched on tiptoe and pressed closer, straining to see. She stepped on her dress, lost her balance, and tumbled into the crowd.

"Watch out, you!" barked a man's voice that just as quickly changed tone. "Oh, beg your pardon, Miss. I didn't mean to push you." A trim, gray-haired man in a double-breasted suit extended his hand and helped Emily to her feet. She flushed, embarrassed that the commotion had drawn the crowd's attention away from the star.

"Emily?" Mr. Chapman pushed his way toward her. "Is that you?"

Emily stared down at the floor. She could hardly breathe as he assessed her with keen attention. Would he reprimand her for borrowing another's dress? For going out alone? If he was upset, he hid his dismay well, instead guiding her with apparent pride back to where Jenny sang.

"Songs my mother taught me, in the days long vanished . . ." Jenny's voice was melancholy. The room, held captive, grew quiet. When she finished, the audience applauded and shouted, "Brava!" What Emily wouldn't give to have people look at her with equal admiration. Someday she would sing like that, perhaps even on a steamboat gliding down the mighty Mississippi.

As the cheers from the audience faded, Mr. Chapman stepped forward. "Ladies and gentlemen, you have just witnessed only a small sample of our many talents. Don't miss our show tomorrow night. Good night, good night. Parting is such sweet sorrow." He swept his hat from his head and bowed, signaling that the impromptu recital was over.

The crowd gradually dispersed, leaving the troupe weary from their day at the mine to make their way to their rooms. But before Emily could join them, Mr. Chapman steered her into a small library near the parlor. She knew it—he was angry, and had held back his reprimand while they were in public. Maybe he would even send her packing back to Saw Tooth City and the Harmons. But instead of scolding her, he kissed the tips of her fingers. "My good Emily, you are absolutely bewitching tonight."

She thought he exaggerated, but was grateful he wasn't upset. She let her hand relax. Kerry Chapman's soft words and attentions warmed her fingers, her toes, and especially her heart. If she had a clock, she would pluck out the hands to keep time from moving forward. Or if she had a book, she would press this moment between the pages; she would do anything to preserve this heady feeling—the way she trembled when he touched her—forever.

CHAPTER EIGHT

Her heart—is given him, with all its love and truth.
OUR MUTUAL FRIEND

EMILY WOKE BEFORE the sun and quietly slipped into her plain and shabby dress. She tiptoed from the room, crept down the stairs, and settled into an inconspicuous chair in a corner where she could watch the boarders come and go. She sensed him before she saw him and looked up just in time to catch Kerry Chapman's gaze. He did not look away; rather, he moved quickly across the room towards her.

"Emily. This is a pleasant surprise." He looked at her intently, and she returned his gaze, unable to move. She tried, but couldn't hide her feelings. She didn't have to look in a mirror to know that her face was one large happy smile. If the leader of the troupe was embarrassed by her unwavering admiration, he did not show it. It seemed to Emily that he was as taken with her as she was with him; he could not look away. She held her breath, wanting to touch him, wanting to make sure he wasn't a dream, until the sleeve of his jacket brushed hers and the slight movement gave her courage.

"I haven't had a chance to properly thank you for all of your kindness." It wasn't what she wanted to say, but at least she remembered her manners.

"Nonsense. You owe me nothing."

"Oh, but I do." A slight tremor began behind her knees, but before it could sway her, she said, "I must repay you. I can't depend on your generosity forever."

He raised his eyebrow and smiled, and she forgot her determination to appear competent. "Please." Her voice was a whisper.

"Let me work for you." She glanced at him for an answer, but dropped her gaze before his eyes met hers. *What he must think of her, standing before him in her short skirt begging for a job.*

"Come," he said. "We shouldn't discuss this in the middle of a doorway." He motioned to a small table near the window. "Please, join me."

They were no longer alone, and the intimacy they had shared turned into a respectable politeness as the room filled with other diners. She allowed him to seat her, and they continued their discussion over a cup of coffee and a plate of toast and jellies.

"Are you sure you want to work for me? You know it isn't necessary," Mr. Chapman said.

"It is. If not for you, then for someone else. Soon. I must find work." She would rather work for him—polish his shoes or iron his shirts—than for anyone else, but she didn't tell him this.

"Well." He smiled and studied her closely. "Seeing you are so determined, we shall see what we can do. Perhaps you could be a lady's maid to Jenny and Bella."

"Yes," she said, too eagerly.

"I hope you enjoy traveling. We never stay in one place long."

"I love to travel." Besides, being away from him—from the senseless way he made her feel when he was near—was unthinkable.

"Then it's settled." He dabbed his lips with his napkin, stood, and offered his hand. "I am delighted to have you join us, my good Emily. Now, I have errands to run. Would you care to assist me?"

"Oh, yes." She folded her napkin and laid it beside her plate of uneaten food, unable to believe her good fortune. Outside the hotel, she took his arm—feeling more than a bit foolish in her short calico dress. She cocked her head to look at him. Was he embarrassed by her appearance? No, it didn't appear so as he smiled and held the door open for her to enter the mercantile.

While he secured the items on his list, Emily lingered over a table of inexpensive fabric looking for a suitable color, enough to make a dress with a proper hemline so she wouldn't look such a child in his presence. She was daydreaming, stroking a bolt of cheap cotton of a garish green, when she heard him say over her shoulder, "Either of these would make a nice dress, don't you agree?" He stood near a table examining several lengths of yard goods that Emily would never dream of purchasing, not even if she were married to the richest man in Vienna.

Before she could answer Mr. Chapman laid a bolt of lavender surah on the counter along with selections of lace, muslin, and navy blue wool. He then instructed the merchant to bring out the latest ladies' shoes—*how had he guessed her size?!*—and watched while Emily tried them on. When he was satisfied with a proper fit, he directed delivery of the majority of the items to Emily's room at the hotel. Done with business, he leisurely led her back across the street. Before he left her, he pressed a coin into her hand.

"Consider this an advance against your first week's salary. Now, go. Buy yourself something frivolous."

Her mouth dropped open with surprise and she stared at the five-dollar gold piece. When she tried to give it back he said, "Please. Take it. I am sure you will earn it. That, and much, much more." He smiled and her resolve faltered.

"Thank you, Mr. Chapman."

"Please. Call me Kerry."

"Thank you—Kerry." The intimate use of his name made her lightheaded.

"You're more than welcome, my good Emily." Sweeping his hat from his head he bowed low and smiled, his eyes so gentle, so compelling, she grew dizzy. With a kiss to her hand, he left her alone with her thoughts and her confusion.

Instead of returning to the mercantile, Emily decided to save the coin. She would not spend it, she resolved, until she had earned it. She slipped the gold piece into a tissue, safe inside her pocket, and returned to her room.

The afternoon passed quickly with mending and preparing costumes for the evening performance. She was glad to have something to do, something to keep her thoughts at bay. If she wasn't careful, she might well lose herself completely to Kerry's seductive smile, his hypnotic dark eyes. Then she never would see the Mississippi River steamboats. Compared to Kerry Chapman, who was very real and very close, the river now seemed far away, merely an abstraction, something she had invented in one of her dreams.

Later, alone with Jenny in the parlor, Emily glanced at the clock on the mantel and said, "Shouldn't we be going?"

"There's plenty of time. Besides, they won't start without me."

While Jenny took her time scratching away at her letter, Emily, wearing one of Bella's yellowed blouses and a long, patched skirt, fidgeted in a chair and daydreamed. She could see herself on stage, singing herself breathless. She could see herself dancing beside Jenny and Bella. Beside Kerry Chapman. A butterfly started in the pit of her stomach and fluttered until she had to move. Such silliness, she thought. Singing. She was nervous enough, knowing she would be assisting Jenny and Bella back stage, behind the curtain. But to sing in public?

"There." Jenny snapped the lid on the inkwell and blotted her letter. She turned to Emily with a bright smile and stood. "Ready? We don't want to keep the good people of Vienna waiting, do we?"

"No, we don't." Emily said. Or Kerry Chapman either.

* * *

The Apollo Hall smelled of fresh paint, green wood, and new velvet curtains. Emily bent her neck to gaze at the golden fresco of the god of music centered directly overhead. With head tilted, she turned. Her eyes traced the long tail of the golden python Apollo squeezed in one of his hands until she had made a complete circle. "It's magnificent," she whispered to no one in particular, expecting no answer.

Imagine, she thought as she followed Jenny and Bella up three wooden steps and onto a large open stage. All this splendor, and tonight she would be part of it. She didn't even have to pay to get in.

She faced the empty auditorium, peering out at the vacant seats, and tried to envision the room the way it would look later, swollen with townspeople. She stared, overwhelmed by the enormous stage and her good fortune.

"Emily? Are you coming?" Bella called, forcing Emily from her daydreams. Giddy and full of anticipation, Emily trailed behind, trying to absorb the very walls as she raised her skirt and tiptoed down the six crude steps that led to the dressing rooms directly under the stage.

Helping Jenny into a long red dress, Emily tried to compare this evening to the first time she'd watched the troupe perform in Saw Tooth City. Then, she had watched the cast parade through town, enjoying the circuslike atmosphere. She had giggled with the audience when Ellerton fell out of bed, struck his head, and forgot his own name. She was still a child then, someone's ward with chores and rules and a future bleak as Dismal Swamp. But here, now, in this fine theater, her future looked brighter. As Emily helped Jenny prepare for the show, she wondered what it would be like to sit in a chair and have someone curl her hair or tie her sash.

She was pinning Bella's torn hem when she heard a scuff at the floor. Without turning, she knew who was there. Kerry's cologne filled the room, overpowering even the smell of Jenny's gardenias. Emily looked up to find him watching her with keen interest.

"Very nice, ladies. Very nice." He walked slowly around Jenny, assessing her like an artist would a painting. Emily watched, wishing he would look at her with the same admiration and pride.

"I must go and see to the rest of the stage props," he said. They joined him backstage, where he gave last-minute instructions. Just before the curtain rose, he looked her way and smiled. Then he was gone. Emily couldn't remember ever feeling so lightheaded, excited, or nervous. She might not know much about performing, but this she knew: she would do everything in her power to be of help, anything to please him.

As she waited behind the curtain with Bella, she was so wound up she thought she might be sick. When Ellerton began the opening song, her mouth turned dry as a riverbed in August, as if the night's performance depended solely upon her. Her hands turned clammy and she looked for a chair before her legs gave way.

Seated inconspicuously behind the curtain, Emily watched the show from the wings. Soon she forgot to be nervous. When Ellerton played a song she was familiar with, she pretended she was singing on stage along with the troupe. She had to turn away when Jenny and Kerry strolled arm in arm across the stage, singing, "You are worth more to me than silver or gold."

The first half of the performance went as rehearsed, following the same format as the show she'd witnessed in Saw Tooth City.

Only this time no one was carried onto the stage on a velvet couch. When the audience applauded, their excitement was contagious. In no time at all, Ellerton's music announced intermission and Emily was busy again, attending to the performers' hair, costumes, and various personal needs.

The second half of the show seemed to move even faster. When Emily peeked from behind the curtain, even more people were packed into the theater. They stood crowded in the aisles and along the back wall. Once again Kerry was charming as the Artful Dodger—so charming he captured Emily's heart completely. She was still dreaming about his performance and forgot herself—forgot the pang she felt earlier when he sang with Jenny—stepping forward when the troupe began their own rendition of "The Homespun Dress," a song Emily now knew by heart:

The miner is the man for me, A brave man I adore,
And when the golden ore is free and mining is no more,
I'll choose me then a lover brave from out this mighty land.
The miner that I love the best shall have my heart and hand.

They had had such fun rehearsing the song and Emily, caught in the moment, brought her hand to her heart and then offered it to the audience. Applause filled the room. Too late, Emily realized what she had done. Blinded by the footlights, she stumbled and tried to run from the stage.

But Kerry was faster. He stopped her, and to her surprise, holding her hand high in the air, led her to the front of the stage. With the kerosene footlights shining on her greasepaint–less face, she was thankful she couldn't see the crowd. *But oh,* she thought, *how awful she must look*. How ashamed he must be.

Afraid to look at the audience and guided by Kerry to the center of the stage, his arm tightly around her waist, Emily bowed. Pulling her closer, he whispered, "Sing."

He nodded to Ellerton and led out on a familiar Stephen Foster tune, "Come Where My Love Lies Dreaming." Emily joined him in the chorus, trying to look only into his eyes and not at the audience. At first her voice sounded weak, like it would dissolve as quickly as sugar in hot water, but by the time they finished the song, her words were clear and her voice was strong. When the number was over, he took her hand, and together they bowed to the audience.

"Bravo! Bravo!" The audience cheered. Emily smiled at the crowd and imitated Jenny as she curtseyed and threw a kiss. When Kerry escorted her from the stage following the audience's thundering applause, Emily felt so giddy she could have been a feather floating on air.

* * *

Downstairs in the dressing room, Emily didn't stop a minute as she gathered dresses, hairbrushes, and ribbons, hoping to reassure Kerry by her actions that she had not forgotten her duties even if she did momentarily misremember her place and made a fool of herself earlier on stage. She must never let that happen again, Emily thought as she tucked costumes into the open trunk, every now and then stealing a glance at Kerry. He smiled at her. Good, she thought gratefully. He was not displeased with her.

"We were magnificent tonight." He exhaled, and blue smoke from a new cigar filled the small room. "We must celebrate. When we get back to the hotel, I'll order a fine bottle of wine. Emily, come here." He picked up the red costume Jenny had tossed to the floor and held it out to Emily. "Go put this on."

The merriment and celebration that only minutes before had filled the room ceased. Ellerton nodded to Brooks, and they made a hasty retreat, leaving behind only the women and their manager. Emily glanced at Jenny. "I couldn't." Jenny stared back, her lips pinched tight.

"If you're going to join us on stage, you must have something to wear." He teased, but his words were kind. He draped the gown over her arm and turned her toward the screen.

Her fingers trembled, and it took her a while to fasten the buttons. Looking down at her exposed bosom, she felt the color rise in her face. Her skin looked too white next to the red lace. She arranged her hair the best she could to cover her bare shoulders and took a deep breath, knowing she no longer looked like a little girl.

"Do you need some help?" Kerry said.

"No." Emily fumbled with the sash and smoothed the dress against her body, hoping she looked as attractive as she felt. When she finally stepped out wearing Jenny's costume, more than her hands were shaking.

"Come. Come here." Emily walked over to where he waited, avoiding everyone's eyes but his. He cinched the fabric around her waist, and she flushed at his touch. "Perfect," he said, stepping back from his creation.

Emily felt naked before the troupe. She turned her head, afraid to look at Jenny, afraid to see resentment growing there like weeds.

Pulling away from Kerry, she slipped behind the screen. In less than a minute she reappeared, fully dressed. She folded the costume neatly and placed it in the trunk the same way she would pack away a dream.

Because she had costumes to mend, Emily stayed behind as the others returned to the Abbott Hotel. Tonight she wouldn't be confined to a boring bedroom. Tonight she wanted to be near Kerry, to feel again the way he held her as they sang their duet on stage. She sat quietly in a corner, mending a hem, while he balanced his ledgers.

"Emily," he said, closing the money box after double-checking his numbers and looking up to see her in the shadows. "Are you still here?"

"Yes," she whispered, putting down her needle.

"Ladies and gentlemen." He stood and pantomimed in a playful mood. "I give you a vision of loveliness with a voice of gold. Emily, our own little Robin of the Rockies." He took her hand, lifted her to her feet, and spun her in circles until she was dizzy.

When she stopped spinning, he drew her close. Instead of pulling away, Emily reached a hand up and touched his face. He bent closer. She tilted her head. Closed her eyes. She wasn't shocked at all when his mouth found hers. And though she had never been kissed like that before, she relaxed, opened her mouth wide and welcomed his tongue, his lips. She welcomed the pleasantly pervasive way he tasted, the profound way he made her reel. Now she had only one wish: that he hold her and kiss her like that forever.

CHAPTER NINE

"There is no use trying," she said; "one can't believe impossible things."
ALICE IN WONDERLAND

SHE TOOK HER CUE from him. When they were alone, which wasn't often, they enjoyed the mysteries of each other: a look, a touch, a kiss. But when they were in the presence of others they behaved cordially, conduct proper for employer and employee. She hid the little gifts he gave her, the trinkets and the baubles. It was harder to hide the clothes.

Through unspoken words, Emily had come to believe it wasn't that Kerry was ashamed of her, or that she was too young to be seen with him. She certainly didn't feel too young when she was in his arms, when his lips travelled slowly from her ear, down her neck, inching closer and closer to her heart. Rather, she believed it was more a matter of propriety. Bella, friendly and helpful before Emily was hired, now seemed sullen and resentful. She watched Emily with a keen eye, often critical of the way a hem was sewn, a bed was turned. So even though Emily preferred she and her beau could have been seen openly and considered a couple, she was cautious and guarded, careful not to give Bella further cause for fault-finding or distress.

Emily noticed that Kerry tried to avoid any semblance of favoritism, although it was clear to her Jenny Starr was his main attraction. It was Jenny's face that graced his handbills, Jenny's voice that closed each performance, bringing audiences to their feet. If he did favor Jenny, Emily didn't mind. She understood it was only business. She was content to perform her duties knowing there would be a time, perhaps later in the day or early in the morning before the others had risen, that they would have a few brief moments alone. It was for those moments she waited.

Sometimes, while she worked, she dreamed they would marry. They hadn't discussed matrimony, but Emily assumed that he was waiting for her to attain her majority. Out West it might be acceptable to be married with a brood of children by age eighteen, but she had read that east of the Mississippi it wasn't proper for a young girl to marry unless she was older and properly courted. Emily blushed at the idea of being courted by Kerry, believing he didn't want to tarnish her reputation by making her a child bride. Still, remembering the way her body responded each time he touched her, she did not know whether she would be able to wait much longer. When she was alone, mending dresses, she rehearsed.

"So nice to make your acquaintance, Mrs. Chapman."

"Please, call me Emily like my dear Kerry does."

"Emily. Such a fine husband you have. He is so courteous, so talented. You must be very proud."

"Thank you. I am. He is my joy, my life."

Emily's spirits were unusually high, having joined in an early morning stroll with Kerry to check on the horses. They had walked properly down the street and exercised discretion until they were alone in the stable, where he pulled her close and kissed her until all reserve was gone. She had wavered, eager one moment, slightly cautious the next, until his kisses convinced her and she willingly succumbed to his advances.

Had he untied her bonnet, or had she? She couldn't remember, but she had straightened her appearance appropriately before he escorted her to the mercantile to secure sundries. After making her purchases, she must have floated all the way back to the Abbott Hotel, because she didn't remember walking.

With a feeling of bliss still lingering, Emily fumbled her packages, trying to open the door to the room she shared with Jenny and Bella. Inside, Jenny was resting, her head buried in the pillow. Bella was gone, perhaps enjoying a late breakfast. Emily untied her bonnet and sorted her purchases. She was putting away a spool of thread when the door opened and Bella entered.

"Thief! There you are! What have you done with my earrings?" Bella pushed Emily's hair away from her face and checked her earlobes. Then she searched Emily's pockets. Finding them empty, Bella said, "What did you do, pawn them?"

"I—I didn't take them," Emily said, shocked Bella would accuse her. "I don't know anything about them."

"Liar. They were on the table last night when I went to bed. When I woke up this morning they were gone, and so were you."

Realizing Bella was like a storm that must blow its course, Emily stood back out of the way and let her wail, feeling guilty in spite of her innocence. When Bella stripped the bed and pulled the mattress to the floor, Jenny intervened.

"Bella, this is madness. Emily didn't take them."

"How would you know, you're always in a stupor."

It happened so fast, Emily had to blink to be sure what she saw was real. Jenny slipped across the room and slapped Bella silent. "Stop your incessant ranting. She didn't take your earbobs."

"Oh, no? Then you explain how one minute they're here and the next minute they're gone. It isn't enough that she wears my clothes. Or 'borrows' my brush and hairpins without asking. Or that I have to share a bed with her. Now she wants my jewelry." Bella pointed a finger at Emily. "And don't think for a moment we don't know what's going on between you and Mr. Chapman. You have your hat set for him, that's for sure."

Emily felt her face redden. "I will never be dependent on some man's arm."

"You would, given the chance," Bella said.

"I would not. But I'll help you look for your earrings," Emily said in spite of her anger and hurt pride.

Bella laughed. "Of course you will. Since you know where you hid them, it makes perfect sense for you to find them."

"Leave her alone." Jenny walked over to the dresser, opened a drawer, and removed her jewelry case. She gave Bella a pair of gold earrings. "Here. Take mine. Now get out of here and let me rest."

Somewhat pacified, Bella accepted the earrings. Before she left the room she said, "You'll be sorry for defending her. Wait and see. My jewelry won't be the only thing around here to disappear."

"Pay her no mind," Jenny said when Bella was gone. "She gets this way. She'll be moody for a day or two, then snap out of it and act as if nothing happened."

How convenient, Emily thought. Even if later Bella did pretend nothing had happened, Emily wouldn't forget. Not for a long, long time. "Jenny," she said, "I swear. I didn't take them."

"I know, Emily. She's misplaced them. Like she always does. Only now she has someone to blame. Don't let her get to you."

And though that might be true, it didn't make Emily feel any better, or lessen her humiliation.

* * *

The troupe had been busy, spending most of each day at the outlying mines. While they were away, Emily had much to do—mending, brushing, and airing costumes. Once, when she volunteered to go with them, Kerry said no, she wasn't ready. That made her peevish, resentful, but she chose to look at it as his way of protecting her. He was only being considerate, trying not to take advantage of her good nature.

Each day the troupe returned from the mines exhausted and subdued. If she were to accompany them, she reasoned, she would be too tired to see to their wardrobe and their needs. So she contented herself, convinced he had her best interests at heart when he left her behind.

But sometimes she wished he wouldn't. She hadn't told him about her growing desire to sing with the troupe. She would like to accompany them on stage. She blushed when she recalled her one and only stage appearance. Perhaps she had embarrassed him with her plainness, and that was why he hadn't encouraged her to join them at the mines. But this seemed odd to her, since he always encouraged her to participate during rehearsals.

Maybe he was just being cautious. Judging by Bella's stormy demeanor, maybe he didn't want to upset the company by including Emily too soon. Or perhaps what he said was true. She wasn't ready yet. Her voice was too childish, not trained enough. So as she worked she practiced, pushing her voice to new octaves, new variations in trills, pretending she was aboard a glamorous steamboat and singing while sunlight shone upon the glorious Mississippi.

It was late when the troupe returned from the Pilgrim Mine. Even in the dim light Emily could see the thin layer of dust clinging to their clothes and hair. Bella removed her duster and Jenny, looking too tired to move, sat on the edge of the bed. "I would give anything for a bath, to be rid of some of this horrid dirt."

Knowing the servants had retired, Emily went downstairs to the kitchen and returned with a teakettle of hot water. Bella was already asleep and Jenny was undressed, brushing the dust from her hair.

"This isn't a bath," Emily said, "but maybe the warm water will help." She poured hot water into the washbasin and added some tepid water from the pitcher. She dipped a washcloth into the water to scrub the back of Jenny's neck. First she unfastened Jenny's necklace to remove it.

Jenny raised her hand. "Don't."

"We don't want to get your locket wet." Emily opened the clasp. "I'll put it right over here. You can put it back on as soon as we're finished."

As she laid the necklace on the dresser, Emily accidentally tripped the lever. The locket sprung open, displaying a picture of Jenny when she was three, maybe four, years old. Her hair hung in long ringlets and her dress was so smart it could have been one of the latest Paris fashions. Emily was sure she had seen a similar frock advertised in one of Mrs. Harmon's *Harper's Bazaars*. She set the locket aside and scrubbed Jenny's neck and shoulders.

"Ummmm," Jenny said. "Now, if only I had my medicine."

Emily gave Jenny the washcloth and while she scrubbed her face, Emily opened Jenny's dresser drawer and took out a brown bottle. Removing the cap, she discovered the bottle empty. This late, the mercantile would surely be closed. She slipped into her shoes anyway, willing to try even though it was long after dusk. "I'll be right back," she said. She pulled a shawl over her shoulders and slipped out the door before Jenny could protest.

A light shone from the back of the building and Emily hurried across the street toward the mercantile, hoping to catch Mr. Riddle before he closed. By the time she arrived, the front door was locked; he was extinguishing his lamp. Unwilling to return to Jenny empty-handed, Emily rapped on the door.

The apothecary recognized her from her many previous purchases for the troupe and unlocked the door. "I'm sorry, Miss Emily. I'm about to close."

"I hate to bother you so late, but we are in desperate need of laudanum."

"I see. I don't think I have any, but we can look." He locked the door behind them and rummaged through an array of bottles and tins he kept behind the counter. When he didn't find what he was looking for, he turned to Emily. "Excuse me for one moment."

Mr. Riddle returned empty-handed. "Just as I suspected. I was sure I had sold my last bottle to Mrs. Dugan this afternoon. I'm sorry, I don't expect another shipment until sometime late tomorrow."

Emily considered her quandary. "Do you know anywhere else I can obtain another bottle?"

"Not at this hour."

"Oh, dear. I really must find some tonight." Her voice weary, filled with tears.

He studied her carefully before he added. "I know of one other place you might inquire tonight, but I would never send a young lady there alone on such an errand."

"Please," Emily said. "This is important. Just tell me where. I'm not afraid to go."

"I'm sorry," he said. "I can't be responsible if something should happen to you." He moved to lock up his store.

"Please." Emily tugged at his arm. "Miss Starr depends on me. I can't disappoint her."

He scratched his chin as he seemed to debate whether or not to reveal the information. "If you can find old Pon Lee," he said with some hesitation, "he should be able to help you. He just opened a house in the new part of Chinatown. I'm not telling you to go there, but if you do, ask for opium pills. Not laudanum." He paused, then added, "See if you can get one of the men to go with you. Better yet, see if one will go for you. A young lady has no place on the streets at night alone."

"Opium pills," she repeated.

"Goodnight, Miss Emily," he said, locking the door behind her.

"Thank you," Emily said. "Thank you so much."

While he watched, she crossed the street and pretended to enter the hotel. When she was sure the druggist was no longer looking, she slipped back out and followed the wooden boardwalk to the end of the block.

Emily looked over her shoulder at the light streaming from the windows of the Abbott Hotel, inviting her back inside where it was safe, where it was warm. She shivered and pulled her shawl closer, then turned and headed south toward Chinatown. She didn't need a sign or a map to tell her where Vienna stopped and Chinatown began—all she needed to do was inhale. The air in Chinatown was sweeter, filled with strange music and aromas, faint with the odor of burning joss sticks, cloves, and ginger. Houses huddled together, putting every square inch of ground to good use instead of sprawling an entire block, as some of the houses in Vienna did. The empty streets were eerie and dark, and she jumped at every sound.

Walking faster, she recalled something Mr. Harmon once said. Chinamen didn't go out at night because they were afraid of the spirits. That explained the empty streets. Emily had never seen a ghost, but just to be safe, she started making as much noise as she could as she hastened through the narrow alleys. If there were any ghosts about, she was determined to make enough noise to scare them away.

She passed a joss house and a small stand illuminated by red Chinese lanterns. She stopped and pressed her nose to the glass windowpane, tempted by the fresh radishes, onions, and lettuce, so uncommon this early in the year. But the door was locked so she walked on, past a laundry where the day's wash still hung from the windows.

To avoid a row of gambling houses, Emily crossed the street again, careful to keep her head down and her footsteps light. From an open window she could hear men speaking in the fast, singsong language she didn't understand. She searched for what she considered the newer part of Chinatown, but the buildings all looked alike. She startled a cat, and it darted away with a screech, carrying what looked to be a fish tail between its teeth. Emily was shaking, ready to turn back, when she discovered the small wooden building with a turquoise sign hanging above the door. Unable to decipher the Chinese characters, she was glad Pon Lee had included the English version of his name.

Unlike the door to the produce stand, this one stood open. Inside, the strange aromas were stronger. She recognized oriental incense from her days at Rocky Bar, and the musty smell of cinnamon and cloves. But there was something else here, something more penetrating. More intoxicating.

When her eyes adjusted to the dim light in the store, Emily noticed a cage with a small window. Behind it were rows and rows of herbs, some of which she recognized, most of which she did not. In one aisle she passed a display of almonds and a table laden with teas and teapots. Colorful kites and paper dragons decorated the ceiling, twirling with the breeze blowing through the open door. She noticed a good selection of sugars and lard, delicate china plates, silk handkerchiefs, fans, and thin red papers as well as a large supply of tobacco and pipes—some made of jade, some of ivory and intricately carved. She passed a basket of oranges and stopped to pick one up. Guiltily, she glanced toward the owner of the store as she remembered how she, George, and Lizzie used to steal oranges from Chinese graves near Rocky Bar and run off to enjoy them under a tree. With a guilt-ridden shiver, Emily set the fruit down while the owner, bent with age and wearing a black tunic, watched. Like many Chinese she had seen before, he wore his hair in a queue that fell down the center of his back. She felt awkward under his gaze and tried to make herself inconspicuous, as if she frequented Chinese stores all the time, as if she knew what she was doing, what she was looking for. She was busy examining an assortment of fragrant teas when he approached.

"You buy?" he asked in broken English.

"No," Emily said. "Actually, I'm looking for lauda— opium pills," she said, remembering to ask for the drug by name.

When Emily said *opium,* the little man nodded and beckoned with an open hand. "Please to follow."

She was nervous, but she was also determined, so she followed him to the back of the store and up a few steps to an area hidden from the public. She wondered where he was taking her, worried if she would have to scream loudly to escape. A silk curtain framed the doorway. Above the door, written on red tissue paper, were several black Chinese figures, and she studied them thoughtfully, as if that alone would help her understand. While she pondered the letters, he pushed aside the silk curtain richly embroidered with red-eyed golden dragons, allowing her to step up into a small dark room.

The room was hazy with guttering tallow candles. She coughed at the pungent odor and smoke from melting wax. As her eyes adjusted, she could distinguish several figures on the floor. Some of them lay on their sides smoking from long pipes, while others rested their heads, nodding as if sleeping. Most of them were Chinese.

He pointed to an empty spot on the floor.

Emily looked at him blankly for a few minutes. "No." She shook her head, feeling the color rise in her cheeks. "To take with me."

He led her to another spot in a corner and pointed to the floor. "No," she tried to tell him, but he appeared not to understand. When he handed her a pipe, she pushed it away.

Her face was warm. It was hard to breathe. "Medicine," she said, trying to show with her hands a small bottle. Now that her eyes had adjusted to the hazy room, she avoided looking at the figures lying on the floor. She wanted nothing more than to be away from this sleep-inducing room.

The old man turned and said something towards the back of the room where Emily could see beds lining the wall, stacked high like cigar boxes. A girl appeared, but not before Emily had a chance to peer into the dark corner, not before she saw that the man lying on the bed was different from the others. He wasn't Chinese; his suit was made of fine material, material she had seen before. Emily looked away, anxious to leave. She repeated her request, and the girl interpreted her words.

"Ah," the Chinaman said, and led Emily back into the store, where he opened a tin can and with a small spoon, began to measure. "How many?"

Emily watched him dip the spoon into a brown mass that reminded her of dark strawberry jam. He put a small spoonful on a piece of thin paper and asked, "More?"

Judging from the small dab on the paper, she would need much more, perhaps the whole tinful.

She pointed to the tin and he nodded, replacing the small daub. He used a wooden abacus to tally her total and said, "Thirteen dollar."

Startled, she thought, surely he jests. But from the look on his face she could tell he didn't. She counted out the money Jenny had given her. Six dollars. Even with the gold piece she kept secure in her pocket, she didn't have enough.

Emily stood straight and laid Jenny's money on the counter. She added her five-dollar gold piece, indicating that was all she had. The man dipped his spoon back into the tin until he had removed what he felt was a sufficient amount. Then he handed her the tin, now only about three-fourths full, and took her money.

Emily grabbed the opium, relieved to be leaving the store. She pulled her shawl tight as she retraced her footsteps, no longer pondering fresh food or laundry and gambling houses. She walked fast, almost ran, making her way back to Vienna. Breathless, she returned to the hotel, holding her aching side.

"You were gone a long time," Jenny said when Emily opened the bedroom door. "I was beginning to worry." In her hand she held open the locket she wore even to bed, and snapped it shut.

"I had to go into Chinatown," Emily said. "No stores were open."

"I'm sorry," Jenny said. "I should have never asked you to venture out so late."

What's done is done, Emily thought, handing Jenny the tin, glad to be rid of it, wishing she could get rid of the lingering smell from Pon Lee's store as easily. "It isn't laudanum, but Mr. Riddle at the mercantile said it's the same thing."

"Thank you, Emily, you're such a dear." And then, as if Emily were no longer there, Jenny opened the closet door and took out a small bundle, which she unwrapped, revealing a pipe, a lamp, and other items similar to those Emily had seen within the past hour in the back room at Pon Lee's. Emily turned her head so she didn't have to watch. She slipped out of her dress and into a cotton nightgown, washed her face, and climbed into bed beside the sleeping Bella. She could hear Jenny scraping the opium from the tin. There was the flare of a match, the smell of burning sulfur, and that odd, bewitching odor that had followed her all the way from Pon Lee's. Emily squeezed her eyes and ears tight, trying not to witness what was happening in the bed beside hers.

It was only after Jenny was settled, breathing deeply into the pipe, and the room became hazy, that Emily remembered. Back at Pon Lee's, lying in a corner assisted by the Chinese girl, she acknowledged what she had seen there. Sure as her name was Emily Ann McIntyre. Hair so blond it was almost white. Even in the darkest shadows of an opium parlor.

CHAPTER TEN

"...if there were no bad people, there would be no good lawyers."
THE OLD CURIOSITY SHOP

THE ROOM WAS HOT. Emily kicked at the covers and floated deeper into her dream.

"Who are you?" A caterpillar with Kerry's smile blew smoke from his hookah with a languid drawl.

"Emily," she replied, waving the offending smoke away with her hands.

"Are you sure?" The caterpillar rolled over onto its back and fell off the mushroom.

"I should be," Emily said, glancing down at her ensemble and recognizing it as one she had sewn with material left over from one of Lizzie's dresses. "What I'd like to know, sir, is who are you?"

The caterpillar put the hookah back into its mouth and inhaled deeply. "One makes you larger than life. Two makes you invisible." Then it crawled off into the grass, leaving Emily alone in the increasing fog.

"Come back," she cried, trying to clear the air by waving her arms. "Kerry, come back." She flung her arms so hard she flogged herself awake.

"What's wrong with you?" Bella yanked the blanket and Emily rolled toward the wall. "If you're going to thrash around all night, get the hell out of here and let me sleep."

Fully roused, Emily slipped from the bed. Pulling a shawl around her shoulders, she curled up in a ball on the rug. But she didn't try to go back to sleep. Instead, she stared at the dark window. At breakfast she would ask him.

She contemplated her dream as the sun rose, streaking the room the color of peaches. It can't be true, Emily thought, turning her head toward Jenny, whose cough had worsened. She could almost hear Mrs. Harmon harp, as if she were in the room standing there beside her. Rotted teeth. Boils and abscesses plaguing the skin. Walking dead.

But, Emily thought, Kerry had none of those afflictions. His teeth were white as bone bleached by the summer sun. He had no noticeable boils. Nor did he walk like a specter. He was very healthy, Emily assured herself. No, Kerry wasn't at Pon Lee's last night. It was only her imagination. Besides, it was too dark to see clearly. No, she decided, she wouldn't ask him. Truth was, she didn't want to know.

* * *

"Giddup." Ellerton flicked the reins and the wagon lurched forward. With a smile big enough to capture the heart of any man this side of the Mississippi River, Emily waved to the enthusiastic crowd trailing the wagon. Even with all of the misgivings growing inside her, she was proud to be part of the cast riding in the wagon instead of a misplaced orphan waving from the dusty road with longing in her heart. The fact that Mr. Harmon hadn't come looking for her gave her hope. Mrs. Harmon must have convinced him not to bother, not to waste his time chasing after someone as lazy as she. Poor Lizzie, Emily thought. She felt sorry for the next orphan they took in with a promise to help, but there was nothing she could do about that now.

When Vienna was no longer a visible speck, Emily turned toward the mountains and looked at the rugged peaks—up—higher until her gaze met the clouds. She was leaving this chain of mountains behind, mountains that surrounded her like a hug. Mountains known to saw a man in half and claim his soul. Tomorrow, she thought with excitement, she would enjoy the commotion of Ketchum, perhaps even stroll the streets arm and arm with her beloved Kerry.

"Proper young women don't venture out unescorted there," he warned her as he told her what to expect in the larger city. "When we get to Ketchum you can't run the streets alone like you did in

Saw Tooth City." She smiled, remembering his reprimand, and took this as his promise to protect her and keep her from harm.

She frowned at how easily her mind settled on Kerry. Not only had he distracted her from her dream to see the Mississippi River and perhaps perform aboard a handsome riverboat, in just a short time her daydreams of him became a habit, not at all unlike his desire for notoriety, perhaps even opium. She looked at him and smiled, satisfied that he was watching her. He smiled back. Her heart beat faster. She turned her attention to the mountains, relieved to be leaving Vienna. And instead of going west towards Rocky Bar, where she knew there were too many opium houses, they were headed east to the modern city of Ketchum where she was sure Jenny—and perhaps even Kerry, although she didn't care to admit this—would be safe from the temptations of evil.

As the wagon jostled down the dusty road, Emily closed her eyes and raised her face to the warm morning sun. Unwilling to let the knowledge gained at Pon Lee's spoil her day, she speculated. Idaho Territory might not be Missouri, but once in Ketchum she'd be miles closer to her dream. Even if she had to dangle her feet in the icy waters of the Big Wood River and pretend the small fishing rafts were riverboats. In any event, she would no longer have to carry water up from Beaver Creek. For this she was grateful—even overjoyed—and she found herself singing. Kerry winked at her and instead of stopping she sang louder, until the rest of the troupe joined in. Even though she still found some of the words troublesome, it was a pleasant enough way to help pass the hours of their journey.

* * *

In Ketchum, Emily found it hard to stay indoors. Jenny and Bella rested, exhausted from the trip over Galena Summit. But Emily was used to the higher elevations—the thin air, the rugged country—and once established in the Palace Hotel, resented having to stay inside. She wanted to put on her new shoes and explore the fine city, but she hesitated. She might have been able to wander the streets alone in Saw Tooth City, but back then—so long ago and far away!—she had been a child. Now she must behave like a lady. So instead of running outside to feel the sun on her face and the wind in her hair, she pulled a chair close to the window and watched the activity on the street below.

From her perch in the two-story building, Emily could see off into the hills, not quite so rugged as those in Saw Tooth City or Vienna, but still high enough to make her feel secure. She turned her head at the sound of gravel under wagon wheels and watched a stagecoach pull to a stop in front of the hotel. A couple with three small children stepped from the coach, followed by an older man dressed in dark clothes, perhaps Reverend Kingsley himself. When she thought the coach was empty, when she was ready to turn her attention to her shoes and bonnet as she was no longer able to sit idle, Emily glanced out the window again, just in time to see a clean-shaven gentleman step from the stagecoach.

Judging from his fine black suit, this gentleman wasn't just another miner struck with gold fever. As he walked toward the hotel she could see that he carried no pick, no gold pan. He had no bedroll, and his leather portfolio looked odd coupled with the wide-brimmed hat perched clumsily on his head. Without the hat, he looked like he could have walked off the pages of Mrs. Harmon's latest copy of *Harper's Bazaar*. Or perhaps if under a different hat—maybe a fur felt top—he could even be David Copperfield himself. Emily watched until the man disappeared. Then, too antsy to remain seated, she slipped into her shoes and hurried down the stairs.

Having selected a Dickens novel from the library, Emily settled into a chair in the lobby not far from the reception desk. She thumbed through the book, hoping it would cure her restlessness. She had just turned the page when she heard his voice. Looking up from her book, she expected to see Kerry. But instead of her beloved, she saw the clean-shaven gentleman from the stage, standing at the desk. When he spoke he sounded just like Kerry Chapman.

"That will be fine, thank you."

Emily glanced around the room to make sure Kerry wasn't there and turned her attention back to the transaction at the desk. The clerk gave the gentleman a pen and turned the register. "You have an interesting accent, Mr. Morrison. Are you far from home?"

"St. Louis," the stranger said.

"Ah, St. Louis. Have me a brother out that way. Hear tell the Mississippi River goes right through St. Louis. Never been there myself, but hope to one day."

The gentleman signed the register while the clerk pulled a key from a peg. "Welcome to Ketchum, Mr. Morrison. I hope you enjoy your stay."

Accepting the key from the clerk, the man slid a piece of paper across the counter. "Maybe you can help me. Have you seen this woman?" Emily stretched her neck as far as she thought polite, straining to see. But all she could discern was a yellowed sheet with one corner missing.

The clerk leaned forward. His brow wrinkled. "Pretty thing," he said. "Your sweetheart?"

"Not exactly," the man hesitated. "More like family."

"I see," the clerk said. "Then I hope you find her. A man needs his family."

The man turned away from the clerk, and for an instant his eyes met Emily's. She felt the color rush to her face and immediately dropped her gaze back to her book. She didn't raise her head again until she was sure he had left the room. Now, no longer interested in reading, Emily was restless beyond sitting still. She felt like running outside where she could breathe. She rose and had one hand on the door ready to push it open when she remembered Kerry's warning about wandering out alone. So instead, she decided to check in on Jenny.

As she climbed the stairs to her room, Emily noticed a piece of paper lying on one of the steps. She picked it up and unfolded it, recognizing it as the one the guest had showed the clerk in the lobby.

One glance at the handbill and her hand quivered. She refolded the paper and pushed it deep into her pocket without reading what was printed in big letters. She didn't have to; the image was already etched deep into her memory. She tried to remember what the stranger had said. A sweetheart? Family? She wasn't sure, but of one thing she was certain: the likeness on the handbill was that of Jenny Starr.

"Emily?"

She turned at the sound of Kerry's voice.

"My darling, you are lovely, as usual." He approached her with a smile. "I see you are rested from our grueling trip. Would you care to join me for a bite to eat and perhaps a stroll?" His suit was immaculate, his white gloves spotless, his smile disarming.

"Yes," she said, happy for an opportunity to be outdoors, happier still to be with him. "Let me get my bonnet." Her feet were light as wings as she raced up and back down the stairs, eager to join him in the dining room.

At dinner shortly afterward in the Palace dining room, Kerry displayed an uncharacteristic spleen. "Watch what you are doing, you incompetent dolt," he barked when a young Chinese water boy, barely as old as George, Emily guessed, spilled Kerry's glass into his lap. Emily flinched. She knew how the boy felt, so frightened, humiliated and cowering. She wished Kerry were more forgiving. But she remained silent, looking down at her plate, as Kerry lectured the boy.

The head waiter approached. "Is something wrong, sir?"

"Oh, no problem at all," Kerry said. "Just a little water. Now," he said with a laugh that eased the tension, "if you would be so kind as to bring me a bar of soap and a towel, I shall most heartedly enjoy my bath."

She watched him turn his smile toward the waiter, at the other people in the room staring at them and thought how quickly he changed his moods. As if tipping a hat, he was warm and charming again, the merry joker. It seemed the man sitting opposite her was very capable of changing demeanor when it suited him. But then, Emily thought, maybe that's what actors do to protect their privacy. Surely acting had its disadvantages, and constantly being polite in public was one of them.

After dining, Emily and Kerry strolled down Leadville Avenue. She inhaled, enjoying the spring breeze and bright warm sun. They turned the corner onto Main Street, and she was amazed how wide the road was, twice the size of the main street back in Saw Tooth City. Wide enough for two carriages to pass without bumping into one another. They came upon a hedge of lilac, mere slips with the exception of one single branch bearing a fragrant sprig of blossoms. With ceremony, Kerry bent to pick the flower.

"Kerry, don't." Emily moved forward to stop him. "It isn't very big. Let it grow."

"Nonsense. Picking one flower isn't going to ruin the bush." He snapped the thin branch in two and with a bow, presented the blossoms to Emily. "For the loveliest of all flowers. Dearest, this is for you."

"Thank you," she mumbled, accepting the sprig. She would rather he had left the young bush alone. The blossoms wilted long before they returned to the Palace, long before she was able to plunge them into a glass of water with hope to revive them.

Later, at the Liberty Theatre, Emily coaxed Jenny's wig into ringlets. Now, when she looked at Jenny, instead of seeing the enchanting, beautiful singer whose visage graced handbills from San Francisco to St. Louis, Emily saw an ailing woman addicted to fame—and opium.

Jenny's eyes were vacant as she watched her reflection in the mirror. Emily felt her own usual enthusiasm replaced with a sense of sadness, a sense of loss. She wondered if she should tell Jenny about the man she overheard in the lobby, the man who had carried her picture all the way from St. Louis like a tin of hope. "Jenny—" she began, but stopped when Kerry entered the room.

"More color," he told Jenny. He turned to Bella. "If you gain any more weight, that costume won't even reach around you. You look like a cow." He tightened her sash, causing her to gasp for air.

"People," he clapped his hands to draw their attention. "It's time." They could hear the piano plink as Ellerton began the opening number.

Emily's heart raced when she heard the music. Someday, that music would play for her. Someday she'd be famous just like Jenny. Even more. But for now, she stepped aside as the troupe headed for the stage.

She was waiting behind the curtain when Ellerton played the music announcing intermission. As the cast vacated the stage, Emily watched the audience clap enthusiastically, then stir, conversing as they waited for the next act to begin. She was on her way to the dressing rooms when she caught sight of the stranger, the peculiar

Mr. Morrison who had brought Jenny's picture with him and dropped it on the stairway.

She moved slightly to get a better look at him and thought it would be nice to have someone admire her like that. So much that he would follow her halfway around the world.

CHAPTER ELEVEN

It was a long and gloomy night that gathered on me, haunted by the ghosts of many hopes, of many dear remembrances, many errors, many unavailing sorrows and regrets.
David Copperfield

EMILY SAT AT JENNY'S FEET, half hidden by the voluminous skirt she was hemming, as the star posed before the mirror and repaired her greasepaint, when they heard a knock at the backstage door. None of the troupe, Kerry included, would have bothered to knock. Before Emily could even get out the words "Come in" the door opened and the man from St. Louis entered. The stranger with the handbill came over to stand right beside Jenny—Jenny, who had become a statue, frozen, holding a tin of rouge near her cheek.

The man nodded. "Jennifer," he said, as matter-of-factly as if he had been exchanging pleasantries across the dinner table with her. Emily's hand slipped, and the needle pricked her finger. Awkwardly, she scrambled to her feet. The man made no move to introduce himself to her.

Jenny's shoulders tightened, but her voice remained calm—broke only a little—when she spoke at last. "Clayton. You're a long way from home."

"So are you," he said. "You don't stay in one place very long either."

Jenny spoke to the mirror rather than to the intruder. "What I do is none of your business." She set the tin on the dressing table. "Emily, my gloves." Then she said to the man she'd addressed as Clayton, "You can see that we are busy. We have a show to prepare for."

"This will only take a minute." The stranger glanced at Emily. "Would you excuse us?"

Jenny replied before Emily could answer. "My friend isn't going anywhere, and I don't have a minute."

The man moved closer. "Make one." The man's eyes challenged Jenny's, and Emily could see they contained more than affection. She wondered whether she should run for Kerry, scream, or perhaps fend off the stranger herself.

Jenny met his eyes in the mirror. "What do you want, Clay?"

"You know what I want. That's why you keep running."

Taking her long gloves from Emily, Jenny tugged them on deliberately one by one, smoothing them over her fingers and up to her elbows. "Who said I'm running?"

The man moved closer, towering over Jenny until Emily was sure he could smell the pomade in Jenny's hair.

"What do you want, Jen? Five thousand? Ten? How much will it take?"

"Get out of here," Jenny said. "How the hell did you get in here in the first place?" She turned to Emily. "Find Mr. Chapman. Now."

Emily stepped forward, but Clayton moved to block her exit. Around the corner, onstage, the music started up, and businesslike footsteps headed in their direction. The stranger backed down. "Jennifer," he said, moving toward the door, "you and I will continue this discussion later."

"My medicine," Jenny demanded when he was gone. "Quick, get my medicine."

Emily poured a dose from a new bottle of laudanum into a glass of water and stirred. "Who is he?"

"Trouble," Jenny said, draining the glass. "Trouble."

Emily wondered just what kind of trouble bothered to follow a person all the way from St. Louis. Judging from the way Clayton Morrison had looked at Jenny, perhaps it was more than trouble. Perhaps it was even love.

* * *

During the evening's performance, Emily kept an eye out for Clay Morrison. Jenny said nothing more about the mysterious intruder.

But Emily was curious. In spite of his rudeness, she wanted to ask him about St. Louis and the Mississippi River. Surely asking a simple question like that couldn't lead a person to trouble. Preoccupied with what she would say to him, she almost overlooked Jenny's growing melancholia. "Emily, my innocent lamb," Jenny said as she fixed her makeup in between songs. "How lucky you are to be young. So unencumbered. Promise me you will be wiser than I have been. Promise me you will never become an actress."

Emily stopped and looked at Jenny. What was wrong with wanting to be an actress with suitors waiting at the stage door with armfuls of flowers, pressing for a word, for a moment of her time?

Jenny's eyes were lusterless. "Promise me you will find a good husband and get away from this madness before it ruins you. "Emily replaced the cap on the laudanum bottle, sure Jenny had consumed another glass of the medicine. "Don't be silly," she said. "Look at how beautiful you are. I want to be just like you. That's all I dream about. Why, people travel for miles just to hear you sing." Even as she said it, Emily knew she was lying. Without her wig and greasepaint, Jenny Starr was anything but beautiful.

"What do you know about dreams?" Jenny said. "You're just a child. Look around you." She turned in her chair and motioned to the dingy walls. "This is the only place where I have any value. Some dream."

Jenny's hand moved to the locket. Then, as if given a cue, she smiled, stood tall, and headed for the stage again. Emily's heart swelled with admiration for her role model. Only a fine actress could put away her problems with a smile and face a room full of people after being so wrongfully abused. Maybe Jenny was right about Mr. Morrison after all. Maybe he was nothing but trouble.

Later, after the show, as Emily helped Jenny with her buttons, Jenny said, "Did you know, Emily, that once I aspired to be a great opera singer? Arrangements were made for me to study with Verdi. I was on my way to Italy."

"What happened?" Emily asked, watching the actress's face in the mirror.

"I was careless." Jenny coughed into her handkerchief, spotting it with blood.

"Come, let's get you home. Bella left ages ago." Emily offered her arm to help Jenny stand, but Jenny pulled back.

"You go. I'd like to sit here a while longer."

"Oh, no," Emily said. "I'm not leaving you here by yourself."

Jenny laughed. "Run along. I'll be fine."

"Here, let me help . . ."

Jenny slapped Emily's hands away. "Leave me alone. I don't need a nursemaid. Emily, really. Sometimes you can be such a bother."

Emily collapsed in a chair, stung. "Then I'll wait."

"Go!" Jenny pointed to the door. "I want to be alone." The hate blazing from Jenny's eyes brought Emily to her feet.

"As you wish." Without looking at Jenny, Emily gathered the soiled costumes and slammed the door. All the way back to the hotel Emily worried about Jenny. *She isn't herself,* Emily argued in her defense. *She's had too much to drink*. She took the soiled costumes to her room, and sat on the bed. *Where was Bella*? Probably off with Brooks and Ellerton, enjoying some well-deserved libations like she always did after a performance. Emily lay against the pillow and tried to rest. But all she could think about was Jenny, and that strange Mr. Morrison. *Fine,* she decided. She'd go back and wait. Jenny would never know.

The building was eerily dark as she pushed the back door open. Lighting the lamp kept on a table near the door, Emily followed the stairs down to the dressing rooms. The men's side was dark, but light streamed from under the actresses' door. Emily stopped when she heard voices. "Come with me." It was Mr. Morrison's voice, the voice that sounded so much like Kerry's.

"You would like that, wouldn't you?" Jenny said. "Then you'll have me right where you want me."

"Jenny." He sounded tired. "I will never have you right where I want you."

Her laugh was half-hearted. "I'm staying here, where I belong."

"If it's about money. . ."

"It isn't about money, Clay. I can't go back."

"She needs a mother."

Who needs a mother? Emily thought. She heard a chair scuttle across the floor and footsteps as Jenny paced the adjoining room. She was sure she should go get Kerry, but she didn't want to leave Jenny alone.

"Find some pretty girl, get married, and go back to St. Louis. Now please leave me. I'm expecting someone and it would be better if you're gone when he arrives."

"Jennifer."

"Go!"

Emily tried to imagine what Clay must look like, having been scorned by Jenny for another. Just when she thought he would beg Jenny to reconsider, she heard him say, "This isn't over."

The door flew open, and he moved swiftly past Emily, up the steps and out the door. There was the sound of glass breaking. Then Jenny started to cry. Emily wanted to go in and comfort the star, but she knew her presence would only make matters worse. Reluctantly she moved from the door, feeling useless and defeated. It wasn't like Jenny could be entertained as easily as Lizzie. A new story or a tickle under the chin wouldn't dry Jenny's tears or fix her broken heart. Some things were just beyond her control.

It was almost daybreak before Jenny entered their bedroom. Bella's snoring kept Emily awake, tossing and turning all night, and wondering if she should tell Kerry about Mr. Morrison. She looked for Kerry at breakfast, but the parlor was strangely quiet. She didn't know the few boarders dining, and she saw no sign of the other troupe members. They were probably all sleeping late, the way they did following a performance. After a light breakfast of toast and coffee, Emily returned to her room. Bella was still asleep. Jenny was standing in front of the mirror, brushing her hair. "Good morning," she said when Emily entered the room. "I'm sorry about last night."

"I'm sorry too." Emily picked up Bella's torn costume and began to sew. "I only wanted to help you."

"I know," Jenny said, putting down the brush and turning away from the mirror. Emily wanted to ask more about Mr. Morrison but decided to leave well enough alone, grateful they could exchange pleasantries after the awful night before. "Well," Jenny said. "I'm off to find something to eat and settle my nerves." Emily watched her leave, and had no desire to follow. After mending the costumes, Emily carried them downstairs, where she washed them outside in a tub behind the hotel, and hung them on a line. While waiting for the costumes to dry, she decided to go for a walk. The fresh air felt good, and she inhaled deeply. Yesterday was a disaster. Today would be better.

She walked a few miles, then circled back to the theater. Finding the side door unlocked, she entered the now quiet building. The once crowded lobby was empty, as was the auditorium. The warm smell of expensive perfumes and hair tonics lingered in the air, and for a moment she could imagine the audience, applauding enthusiastically for Jenny.

Certain no one was watching, Emily stepped onto the stage. She pantomimed the words to the songs and curtsied to the make-believe audience. At the end of her performance, she threw a kiss to the silent hall. *Someday,* she thought as she left the stage and descended the stairs to the dressing rooms. *Someday they will applaud me, too.*

As soon as her feet hit the bottom step, she smelled something heavy and sweet. Opium? She pushed against the door to Jenny's dressing room. "Oh!" She stopped and gaped.

Jenny was reclining on a couch, in a disgraceful state of undress. Her dress lay on the floor along with her corset and stockings. Emily was ready to enter the room when the sound of his voice stopped her. "For the loveliest of all flowers. Dearest, this is for you."

Emily recognized the voice and the very words she had heard earlier, when he had presented her with a sprig of lilac. Her hands turned cold and even though she knew she shouldn't be watching, she couldn't make herself look away. In the shadows where they couldn't see her, Emily watched as he passed the opium pipe to Jenny. He kissed her ears, her neck, her——. Emily's throat constricted. "No!" She brought a hand to her mouth to stop the words, but they had heard her.

"Who's there?" Kerry demanded. He stepped into the hallway, then returned to the room. Emily remained still, unable to breathe.

Ashamed and humiliated, Emily put her hands over her ears and tried to watch the floor. He was moving back to Jenny. She was in his arms. They were kissing. As soon as Emily felt it was safe to leave without being detected, she raced from the theater, putting distance between herself and that horrid place. "Liar!" she screamed as she ran. Tears blurred her vision, causing her to trip. People stared as if she carried a deadly disease, and they veered away from her before she could infect them.

She ran through town and hid in the woods. She sobbed until her throat ached. Never before had she cried so hard or felt so miserable. Not even when the children in Rocky Bar made fun of her mother and called her the mining camp whore. Emily sniffed. If her mother was a whore, what did that make Jenny? She sat a long time, staring at the road and the trees. She knew this country; she was safe here. Emily looked at the mountains. She had strong legs. She could make her way back to Saw Tooth City. It wasn't that far.

No! She was never going back there. Or to the Palace Hotel either. She stood and started to walk, but she could still see them, Jenny and Kerry groping each other in an opium fog. Emily flinched. Kerry Chapman was far from the man she imagined. Further still from that summer promise. Her body shook, and she struggled to control the pain rending her heart.

She walked. And walked. Until her feet were blistered. Until her face was dry, and she had decided what she must do.

CHAPTER TWELVE

"Would you tell me, please, which way I ought to go from here?"
"That depends a good deal on where you want to get to," said the Cat.
"I don't much care where—" said Alice.
"Then it doesn't matter which way you go," said the Cat.
ALICE IN WONDERLAND

INSTEAD OF RETURNING to her room, Emily stopped at the desk in the Palace Hotel and asked the clerk, "I'm looking for Mr. Morrison. Do you know where I might find him?

"No ma'am," the clerk said. "Perhaps you will find him across the street." She found him sitting at a small table by a window in the restaurant and approached him, back straight and voice clear. "Mr. Morrison," she said, "may I have a word with you?"

Clayton Morrison looked up from his dinner.

She offered her hand in introduction. "Emily McIntyre." When he stood to take it she immediately felt like a child of ten.

"Yes, I recall our earlier—meeting. What can I do for you?"

"If I could, I would like to talk to you about St. Louis."

"Sit down, then." He motioned to a chair and held it while she was seated. "What do you want to know about St. Louis?"

She folded her hands firmly on top of the table to keep them from shaking. "I . . . I have relatives there I would like to locate." She felt the color rise in her face at the lie but pressed on.

"And how can I help?"

"Well," she hesitated. "I have never met them." That, at least, was the truth.

"And?"

Her face grew warmer. "Oh, I don't know. This was a mistake." She pushed her chair away from the table, as if to rise.

When she'd hatched her plan, it made perfect sense. She would ask him to take her along. She would find work in St. Louis and repay him. But now her plan sounded stupid. Why should he help her? He might not even be returning to St. Louis. He could be headed to Oregon or San Francisco for all she knew. She should leave before she made more of a fool of herself in front of this stranger.

"Miss McIntyre, please sit down." He studied her with an even gaze until she was settled. "These relatives I assume, still live in St. Louis?"

"Yes, I think so." She kept her voice calm.

"Would you like me to write some letters, check the county records for you, when I return?"

Movement near the door caught Emily's attention. She slouched into her chair as Kerry and Ellerton entered the parlor. She turned her head, hoping Kerry wouldn't see her. She didn't move until he was settled with his back to her at a table far across the room. Then she rose, almost in a panic. "I have to go."

Clay's eyes flickered from the actor back to Emily. "Has he harmed you?" he asked, keeping his voice low.

"Yes. No." The sight of the rogue chased away her rational thoughts, and she shivered. She wasn't sure whether it was pain or anger that made her hands shake so. She was only sure she never wanted to see him again. Painfully she acknowledged that she would never find herself in Kerry Chapman, but rather in the choices she made, beginning that day.

"Come with me," Clay said. "This way." He stood and enveloped her with a guiding arm that shielded her until they were safely away from the parlor. In the corridor, he said, "You want to leave here and travel to St. Louis, I'm guessing?"

Emily nodded her head vigorously. "I'm catching the eastbound morning stage. Come along if you wish."

"I would like that very much," she said. "But I have no money. I've lost—"

"Let that be my concern, Miss McIntyre. You'll not worry for your fare or meals."

"Thank you, thank you!" She grabbed his hand.

"Tomorrow," he said untangling his hand from hers. "Meet me in front of the stage bright and early tomorrow."

* * *

Emily avoided the hotel room until Bella and Jenny left for the theater. Then she slipped in and quickly fetched her tin box. For a minute she was tempted to take the new dress and corset folded neatly in her dresser drawer, along with the other items Kerry purchased for her and Bella's hand-me-downs in the bargain. But she left them all behind, knowing she would never be able to wear them again without thinking of Kerry or his betrayal.

She dashed a note for her roommates, which she hoped sounded lighthearted and convincing, saying she'd met up with the Harmons from Saw Tooth City and would spend a day or two with the children while they were in town. She assured them her chores were caught up, the costumes were outside drying on the line, and promised to be back. She left the note on the bureau, then departed the Palace for good. Her last remaining coins would buy her dinner and a bed at a small boarding house far from Main Street, far away from Jenny and Kerry.

* * *

The next morning Emily stood, fidgeting, outside the Gilmer & Salisbury stage line station waiting for Clay to arrive. *St. Louis,* Emily thought, her stomach aflutter. *She was actually going to St. Louis.*

"Good morning." Clay greeted Emily, carrying his leather portfolio, a valise, and a satchel that looked a lot like Jenny's, and her nerves calmed a bit. Nothing, not even the thought of Jenny, could spoil her excitement now, and she bit her lip to keep her enthusiasm at bay. She looked down at her dress, her worn shoes, knowing they would have to do. The only thing she carried was her tin box. She followed Clay to the window, where he instructed the clerk. "I would like two seats on your next coach to Blackfoot. One for me and one for my niece."

Niece? Emily thought, looking behind her.

"That will be thirty-six dollars." The clerk handed Clay the tickets. "Our next stage leaves in fifteen minutes. We're already boarding."

Clay handed his luggage to the coachman and turned to Emily. "Wait here. I'll procure a couple of box lunches for the trip."

"But . . ."

"But what, Miss McIntyre. Have you changed your mind? You don't want to go?"

Emily struggled for the right words, resenting whatever it was about him that made her feel small, like a child who didn't know which to choose, the lemon drop or the licorice. "What niece?" she finally managed to say.

Clay laughed at her confusion. "You, my dear," he whispered. "You are my niece."

"I am not." She took a step back.

Taking her arm, Clay gently tugged her away from the window. "You are now. Unless you want people to think you're a fallen woman."

Her face was warm, her palms sweaty. She looked at her feet. "I don't understand."

"Well, Miss McIntyre. It's improper for a young lady to accompany a man in public unless the two are related or betrothed. Therefore, until we get you properly established in St. Louis, you are my ward."

She watched him cross the street and enter Pinkham & Leonard's general mercantile. If it was improper for her to be seen unchaperoned in public with a man, what had the people of Ketchum thought of her strolls with Kerry? Her face burned with humiliation.

She turned her back to the store. Things were a lot simpler in Saw Tooth City, where everyone knew each other and you didn't have to lie about who you were just to take a walk. She realized the first thing she would have to do once she reached St. Louis was locate a good book on etiquette. Apparently they did things differently in the East.

She waited five minutes, ten. Knowing the rest of the passengers were now seated, Emily began to worry. If only he had given her a ticket she could be boarded, ready to leave with the stage. She looked towards the mercantile. If he didn't hurry, the stage would leave without them.

The head driver yelled down to Emily. "Where's your Mister? We gotta be going. Can't wait any longer."

She had just about decided to board, Clayton Morrison or not, when the head driver raised his whip. The horses flinched, causing the stage to rock. Startled, Emily stepped back out of the way as the stage lurched forward.

"Wait!" Clay yelled, clutching the lunch boxes. He chased the stage until the driver stopped. Surrendering the tickets, he helped Emily into the coach.

The coach was so crowded they had to sit on the center seat, which meant they had nowhere to rest their backs and little room for their feet. But Emily didn't mind. Even if she had to stand all the way to St. Louis, she was happy to be aboard, happy to be leaving Idaho Territory, the tragic Jenny, and the deceitful Kerry.

As soon as Clay sat down, the coach lurched forward, this time without stopping. Emily had been inside a stagecoach before. But only while it sat empty, outside Belden's store, waiting for mail and passengers. Now it was almost impossible for her to hide the way she felt about her good fortune. She turned her head to take in the assorted travelers, eight including her and Clay. In one corner sat a gray-haired priest—at least she took him for one, from the crucifix he wore around his neck and the way his head bent over a prayer book. Another passenger, a man with hardly any eyebrows like Uriah Heep, wiped his hands on his handkerchief and lit a cigar. She watched as he blew the disgusting smoke up toward the ceiling with a grin, revealing a large gap between his yellow front teeth.

Emily held one hand to her mouth and tried not to cough, tried to push away the memories of Kerry the man evoked with his smelly cigar.

As they neared the noon hour, the aroma of fresh baked bread and salted meat wafted from opened lunch boxes, fusing with the strong smells of tobacco, leather, and dust. The stagecoach jarred over the gravel road and Emily's stomach turned. She bit her lip, praying she wouldn't get sick.

Boorish, blowing smoke into the dusty air, the man disregarded anyone else's comfort but his own. Grossly overweight, he seemed to take pleasure in making Emily uneasy with his intrusive leers as he squirmed in his seat, crowding the Father further into the corner.

The Father looked like a gentle man. He reminded Emily of Reverend Kingsley, only his eyes looked kinder, like he would preach milk and honey along with his fire and brimstone. If she had to travel with a poor imitation of Uriah Heep and a man who sounded just like Kerry who Jenny called trouble, it gave her comfort knowing at least one person aboard was a man of the cloth. That one of them, at least, she could trust.

The coach jostled, and Uriah Heep smiled at Emily. She tried to ignore him, but every time she looked up, he was examining her as though she were a leg of mutton at market. His fancy pressed suit smelled like it just came from the Chinese laundry and she couldn't wait for the stage to stop, for him to vacate the coach. Hoping the obnoxious passenger wouldn't be making the trip all the way to Blackfoot, she gripped the straps on the floor until her fingers grew numb.

With a lurch, the coach jarred and Emily slipped, falling into Clay. Had the door been open, they would both have tumbled out onto the ground. He saved them by putting his hand out, bracing it against the floor.

"Whoa!" The driver shouted. There was a loud snap, like timber breaking, and the horses stopped, leaving the coach pitched at a strange angle. Emily had to hold onto her seat to keep from sliding to the opposite side of the coach and into the disagreeable gentleman.

When they stopped completely, the head driver poked his head inside. "Slight accident, folks. Looks like we snapped a wheel. It'll take a spell to fix it. Y'all want to get down and stretch your legs."

Emily was glad for the opportunity to get out of the stuffy coach, away from the crowd and stench. With Clay's help, she stepped down and made her way toward a small stream, anxious to wash her face and get a much needed drink. Believing herself alone, Emily bent down and dipped her hands into the cold water. Taking a long drink she turned, then sputtered, spilling water down the front of her dress. She pitched forward and had to put a hand out to keep from falling into the stream. "You startled me," she said, trying to catch her balance as water dripped off her chin.

"I thought you might be hungry." Clay extended his hand to help her stand.

Her wet hand slipped into his, and once again she felt small.

When her feet quit wobbling, Emily settled on a grassy spot near the stream and opened the box he gave her. In spite of the dust and the unpleasant morning ride, Emily found she was hungry and she had to remind herself to eat slowly, like a lady.

Presently, he nodded in the direction of their corpulent fellow passenger. "You don't suppose we will have to endure his good company on the train to Ogden, do you?"

She choked on her sandwich. Ogden? Never once had it crossed her mind that the man wouldn't stay in Blackfoot, at the end of the stage line. She had been counting on it. But of course he would be going on to Ogden, just like they would. What kind of business would an important-looking man have in Blackfoot?

Emily mulled this new revelation while they ate their meal in silence. She was pleased Clay thought to include a bottle of lemonade, which she swallowed in one long drink. She saved the peppermints she found in the bottom of her box, thinking she would enjoy them later.

Having finished her lunch, Emily stood and brushed the crumbs from her skirt.

"Shall we?" Clay offered his arm, indicating a walk along the stream. He stood so close she could feel his breath on her shoulder, his words in her hair.

"Mr. Morrison," she said taking a step or two away from him, "when we get to St. Louis we will have to work out some kind of arrangement where I can repay you."

Drawing her closer he said, "I've already given that some thought, and I have a proposal." He looked at her intently, as if her price were stamped in red on her forehead.

Crimson rushed to her face. Pulling free, Emily said, "I'm not interested in keeping your bed warm." If she had wanted to become a prostitute, she would have stayed behind in the mining camps. She would have moved in with her mother. She walked faster, trying to put distance between them.

"Don't be foolish." He matched her stride. Then turning as if arguing a case and she were the jury, he put out his hand and stopped her. "At Lafayette Manor we have a spirited young girl, six years old to be exact, who needs guidance. I have spoken with Jenny, and she tells me you are good with letters and numbers. As well as children. She believes you would make a good companion for Betsy."

She took a step back as if he had slapped her. Why would he be discussing her with Jenny? She turned away from him. If Jenny had recommended her, Emily wanted nothing to do with his proposal. "I'm sure there are many better qualified in St. Louis than I."

"That may be," Clay said close at her side. "But I made Jenny a promise and I intend to keep it."

Since he stood directly in front of her, Emily couldn't escape. But where would she run, here in the wilderness, anyway? She was miles from Ketchum, and too far to walk back to Saw Tooth City. She looked at his face and even though she saw genuine concern and no disdain, she knew she must refuse. No, she could not accept his offer even though she was sure she could handle the position; at ten she could read and keep accounts. But she had already made one stupid mistake. She wouldn't complicate her life by making another. Not if Jenny was involved. Just the idea made Emily ill. She moved into the sun, seeking its warmth.

"Give it some thought," he said, stepping out of her way so they could continue their walk.

They walked for a while in silence until Emily stooped, picked up a rock and examined a small gold fleck running through it. "There must be something else I can do," she said. "I could hire out as a maid or a cook."

"You could," he said, "but it isn't necessary. You will have plenty to do tending Betsy."

She held her hand up to block the sun shining on the gravel in the stream. "Fool's gold," she said tossing the rock back into the water. Fool, just like her. She turned and faced Clay. "Mr. Morrison, I'm sorry, but I can't . . ."

He grabbed her arm so abruptly she tumbled forward. "Why are you fighting me on this? Would you rather I send you back to Ketchum?"

Struggling to regain her balance Emily said, "I don't need Jenny's help. I don't want anything to do with—"

He interrupted her before she could make a bigger fool of herself by explaining. "Jenny won't be a problem. She has her magnificent career to pursue."

Emily looked up at the tone in his voice. It was the first time she'd heard bitterness creep into his words. But he had turned his face, and she was too late to see his frustration.

I know how you feel, she thought, sharing his disappointment. He had traveled halfway across the country to see Jenny, and she had ordered him away, dismissed him like a simple servant.

Well, Emily debated. She wouldn't behave as badly as Jenny. She would do as he asked. She would console this child Betsy for a month or two, until the child was old enough for boarding school. Then Emily would be free to pursue her own future. Of course she'd have to work, but while she worked she could take voice lessons. Maybe one day she could sing on one of those fancy riverboats.

Emily looked down at her hands. No, maybe she'd find something else to do besides sing. She didn't want to be another Jenny, not ever. She consoled herself that this child, this Betsy, was really Little Nell forced to sleep on ashes for warmth. She could see herself as some sort of savior, settling all the injustices forced upon Little Nell and her grandfather. In that way, her role wouldn't be so different from Clay's, who was right this minute saving her from a disastrous alliance with Kerry.

They followed the stream until they came to a cluster of daisies. Bending down, he picked a flower and offered it to her. "Miss McIntyre, will you accept my offer?"

"I will," she said, accepting the daisy. She held the blossom to her nose, breathing in its delicate fragrance, remembering the young lilac bush Kerry destroyed in Ketchum. Clutching the daisy, she was sure she was making the right decision.

"Good," he said. "I'm glad that's settled."

The other passengers had already gathered around the coachman, who was just tightening the band on the wheel as Emily and Clay approached. "Wheel's fixed, folks," the coachman said. "Time to roll. We have a couple of hours to make up. "After the passengers had boarded Emily settled into her seat, wishing now she had something to lean her head against. With her stomach full and the sun beating down, hot even with the leather shades fastened, she felt her eyelids droop. She fought hard to stay alert. Her head nodded and she jerked herself awake, only to find her face inches from Clay's chin, close enough to see the marks left by his razor. Her first impulse was to move a proper distance away, but she didn't. Half asleep, she was comfortable. And though she knew better, she closed her eyes, prepared to doze as the coach rattled toward Blackfoot. *I must be truly mad,* she thought, fighting sleep. To go east with a man I know nothing about. She didn't even know where she was going—only to some vague Lafayette Manor in St. Louis, Missouri.

A sense of panic swept through her, and she tried to push it away. She sat up, shaking her head, trying to put some distance between them on the narrow seat. If she had learned anything from her relationship with Kerry, it was that trusting someone she hardly knew turned her head into mush and made her stupid. And she'd never be stupid again.

So even though she would like nothing better than to settle against his shoulder and let her drowsy eyes close again, she forced herself to stay awake, to stay as far away as she could from this man Jenny called trouble.

St. Louis! She turned her attention away from the man to her destination. She could hardly believe her good fortune. As the coach jostled down the dusty road toward Blackfoot, she thought, *Emily Ann McIntyre, I hope you know what you are doing.*

CHAPTER THIRTEEN

"...I hope for better things. I will pray for them, and believe that they will arrive."
DOMBEY AND SON

"YOUR BAG." CLAY HANDED Emily the satchel that looked a lot like Jenny's.

Standing outside her bedroom door at the Keeney House in Blackfoot, Emily eyed the bag suspiciously while the proprietor opened the door and set a lamp on the table.

"Your room, Mr. Morrison, is this way, right across the hall."

"Good night," Emily said, and closed her door. The room wasn't as big as the one she'd shared with Jenny and Bella in Ketchum, but it was clean, with fresh water, soap, and towels on the washstand. There was even a spring bed in the corner. It was the first time Emily had had such a fine room all to herself, and she felt a little giddy. She scolded herself, *Emily, you mustn't let this go to your head. This is simply a room many people have used before you*. Nonetheless, as she scrubbed the day's dust from her hands and face and dried off with a towel she didn't have to use after Jenny or Bella, she couldn't help but smile. She was indeed blessed—a room she didn't have to share, a room she didn't have to clean.

Only then, in private, did she dare open the satchel. Inside she found all the garments she'd determined to leave behind: her corset, her new dress, Bella's hand-me-downs. Jenny must have packed it and sent it with Clay. Unfolding the dress brought back every regret and unpleasant memory of Ketchum, and she shoved it back into the bottom of the bag.

Setting aside a flannel nightdress, she continued to repack the satchel when she discovered Jenny's scarf. Thinking Jenny included it by mistake, Emily was folding it to tuck back into the bag when a five-dollar gold piece fell to the floor. She picked it up with wonder. Now the excitement she felt over her trip to St. Louis was replaced with sadness.

Emily slipped into her nightgown and into the bed. She fell asleep wondering where Jenny had gotten the money. Was she frantically missing it now—to purchase the drugs she could no longer live without—or had she meant it as a repayment, or a gift? "There's a lot about you, Miss Jenny Starr," Emily whispered as her eyes closed, "that I clearly don't understand."

* * *

At the station the next morning, Emily's stomach churned with excitement. She could hardly believe her good fortune. To think, her very first encounter with an Iron Horse! And they'd be able to say good-bye to the stage once and for all.

Her enthusiasm faded once she boarded the train, however. Inside, the cars were crowded, with no plush chairs to lean back in, only straight narrow benches. Only small kerosene lanterns sufficed for light. This train was nothing at all like the pictures she'd seen in Mrs. Harmon's magazines. Posted above each door were signs that read BEWARE OF FIRE.

"Would you prefer a seat near the window?" Clay asked, pointing to one of the benches.

"Please," she said.

Once they were seated and the train was moving, Emily pressed her nose against the window, eager to watch the passing scenery. She soon tired of the unchanging desert terrain—the miles of flat, barren land dotted dusty-gray by an occasional sagebrush.

The sparse landscape outside the window became monotonous. Her head nodded and her eyes closed. She began this journey prepared to see something more than pine trees. Now she could confirm that mountains were much more engaging than miles and miles of wasted land, even if it was springtime and occasionally she could spot lupine or a patch of yellow mule's-ears outside the window.

Rays from the afternoon sun blazed through the window, making it impossible for Emily to get comfortable on her hard, narrow seat. No matter how many times she changed positions, her back ached. If she sat in one position too long her legs began to numb. Having switched places with Clay earlier in the day, now she had to lean over if she wanted to look out the window, which she didn't. She even wished Clay would close the blinds and block out some of the dust sifting into the cramped car like stale flour, making her sneeze.

Longing for a cool mountain breeze, Emily glanced at Clay, his coat properly buttoned tight even in the heat. In spite of the constant jostle, he sat up straight, his back solid as a board. His jaw was tense; his eyes never wavered from the periodical he held. Yet, she noticed, he hardly ever turned a page.

What could be duller than the scenery, Emily wondered, leaning closer to see what he was reading. Certainly something to do with the courts, maybe a legal document? Instead she read, *The Resources and Attractions of Idaho Territory.*

He was right to be bored with the booklet, Emily thought. There was nothing interesting in Idaho Territory unless it was the expanding train routes. She fidgeted, wishing she had a book to read, wondering if Mrs. Harmon remembered to return Bobby Pierson's copy of *Oliver Twist.* What she wouldn't give to have a book with her now to help pass the warm afternoon.

"Excuse me." Clay stood, still holding his booklet, and walked down the narrow aisle towards the back of the car. Emily slipped into his seat and looked out the window. Seeing nothing but the endless, dreary sagebrush, she dropped the blind and sighed. Her legs were cramped and she would not mind walking the aisles like Clay, but she was afraid the rocking and pitching of the train would throw her off her already unsteady feet. She was used to having the ground stay put under her legs instead of moving at twenty-five miles an hour.

Staring at the empty bench in front of her, Emily planned her future. Ogden, she thought. Omaha. And then St. Louis.

* * *

The sun was low in the west, streaking the horizon a brilliant orange with soft purple hues, when the train arrived at Ogden Junction. Western terminus of the Union Pacific and Central Pacific Railroads, Ogden was wild with confusion as Emily stepped from the train. She'd never imagined such chaos or snorting locomotives. Cranky brakemen hitched and unhitched cars, preparing for trips east and west, north and south. Pyramids of Saratoga trunks and satchels toppled along the wooden platforms while baggage expressmen wrangled and swore over unmarked luggage and transfers. With only an hour to move their luggage and get something to eat, Emily watched anxious passengers struggle baggage left and right, scurrying like ants overturned by a badger.

As Clay tended to the transfers, Emily wandered down the platform toward two brown bears performing tricks at their trainer's instruction, begging food from people and straining against the long, heavy chains binding their hind legs. Emily watched as spectators petted the bears and dropped coins into a shiny tin cup before turning away. She, too, was tempted to pet the animals—only cubs—but wondered if they were dangerous. She'd seen bears before in the mountains, but the only bear she'd ever touched had been quite dead. Its pelt hung in the Rocky Mountain Tavern, back in Saw Tooth City, with its mouth open wide, teeth and claws bared as though ready to attack.

Emily wandered away from the bears, down a street lined with candy stores and hotels—all kinds of establishments catering to tourists. She forgot time and meandered with the rest of the people, gawking at the many luxuries—pretty bars of soap, blankets, and sweets like none she had ever seen before—offered for sale. She was several blocks from the terminal when she heard the whistle. Emily turned to make her way back to the train, realizing with a start that nothing looked familiar. Quickly, she searched for the confection house, the Z.C.M.I. store she saw on the corner. Somewhere she had taken a wrong turn, and instead of walking closer to the train depot, she was going farther and farther away.

The train whistle blew again, this time fainter, and Emily panicked, recalling a story she overheard Mrs. Harmon tell one of the boarders about a young girl lost in San Francisco. When they finally found her, she was working as a prostitute, having been sold into white slavery. Frantic for a familiar landmark, Emily wiped her sweaty hands on her dress, thinking once again that if she had wanted to be a prostitute, she would have stayed in the mining camps.

Before, whenever she lost her way in the mountains, she only had to look up toward Abraham's Chair to know which direction to go. Now Emily looked up, but looking at this sky didn't help. Even though the sun had set, the stars had yet to appear. There was nothing in the sky to help her find her way. She thought she heard the rumbling of the train and ran toward the noise, bumping into pedestrians as she moved. She turned a corner and there in front of her was the man from the stage, the man with the cheap cigars. He recognized her and turned in her direction, but she rushed past him before he could put a hand out to stop her. She ran toward the dwindling crowds until finally she reached the terminal.

Relieved to reach a familiar place, Emily slowed her pace to catch her breath. She even looked over her shoulder to make sure she hadn't been followed. As she approached the platform, she saw Clay's tall figure searching the crowd, a worried look on his face. When at last he spotted her, his face turned white. With long strides, he hastened to her side.

"What were you thinking, wandering off alone!" His hand on her arm was unyielding as he pulled her toward the train like a father dragging a disobedient child.

"I…"

He stopped in the middle of the crowd and shook her. "This isn't Saw Tooth City, Emily. This is Ogden. You can't wander off by yourself in large cities. Doing so could mean death. Or something worse."

"I'm sorry." He had a right to be angry. Emily still shook from her near encounter with the offensive man. Clay's touch was firm as he pushed her up the steps into the train. The color didn't return to his face until they were seated and safely on their way. She did wonder why her welfare seemed to concern him, though. What did her safety matter to him? She could disappear from the face of the earth, and no one would come looking.

"In the future," he said.

"In the future," she interrupted, smoothing her dress and retreating from his stronghold, "I'll be more circumspect." She settled into her seat and looked out the window, knowing if she was to survive in the East on her own, she would have to be more careful.

As the train rolled toward Omaha, Emily felt her excitement growing. Leaving the small narrow-gauge cars behind and settled in a fancy Pullman was like stepping off a dusty road into a grand hotel. She'd never seen such handsomely carved furniture, black walnut polished to look like obsidian, with plush velvet seats. The walls were inlaid with exotic woods; glass chandeliers glowed overhead. If she were a modeler, she could very well be in one of Mrs. Harmon's magazines, headed east on a train.

She wouldn't miss the narrow benches they left behind in Ogden, that was for sure. She settled into her overstuffed seat and stroked the lavish velvet. Her earlier disappointment in the emigrant cars was replaced by enthusiasm as she tried to see herself as Lizzie would, riding on an Iron Horse, and she had to fold her hands to keep from clapping. She leaned back into the velvet and grinned. Most of the people she knew had never even seen a train, let alone ridden in one.

Emily glanced at the man beside her, his jaw set firm, and thought about the job waiting for her in St. Louis. Her heart beat a little faster when she thought about Betsy and she worried she wouldn't know how to deal with a young girl from the East. She might know her numbers and her letters well enough to teach, but she knew nothing about being a companion, or eastern attitudes and polite society. She shifted in her seat. Funny about life, she thought, trying to study Clay from the corner of her eye without being noticed. You never knew just where it would lead you. And now, thanks to Clay Morrison, it was leading her east, straight to the Mississippi River, to St. Louis, and her future.

They rode along in silence and though he sat close enough for Emily to touch him, he seemed miles and miles away. Wondering what he was thinking, Emily turned her attention to her hands, now not quite so callused, now more like Jenny's. But when she thought about Jenny she thought of Kerry, and sadness invaded her like an affliction. So instead of dwelling on the past, Emily put her mind to appreciating her present surroundings. She studied the railroad car, trying to memorize every detail. She wished she had paper so she could record every chair, every window, so she wouldn't forget her lovely accommodations. But she didn't, so she put herself to watching the women playing whist in a corner near a window and the men in fine business suits striding the aisles in search of smoking cars.

Rising, Emily had just decided to visit the dining car when the train jolted to a stop. "What's happened?" she asked, falling back into her seat.

"Wait here," Clay said. "I'll find out." She watched Clay walk toward the front of the train and thought how different he was from Kerry. When he moved there was no flurry, no bravado calling a crowd's attention. Just an ordinary man seeing to business. It was a while before he returned and when he did, he said, "We've hit a cow. The crew is busy now, trying to disengage it from the cowcatcher."

"Will it take very long?" Emily asked, wondering what a cowcatcher looked like. She imagined a man on horseback swinging a rope.

"It could take a couple of hours. Would you like to leave the train, maybe stretch your legs? You can if you promise not to run off again."

She nodded, refusing to give him the satisfaction of a smile.

With the news of the accident, the car filled with commotion as many of the passengers disembarked to see for themselves. Emily, too, was curious but couldn't get close enough to see the mishap. Clay, at her side, tried to guide her away from the carnage, which suited her just fine since she was more interested in what lay beyond the crowd. Eagerly, she followed the tracks, heading east, but all too soon he said, "Emily, we should go back."

She put her hand up to shield her eyes and looked ahead. "Is it far to the next terminal? Could we walk?"

"Walk?" he laughed. "There are snakes out here."

"If it's going to take hours to clear the track, maybe we should walk. We could get there sooner."

"Don't be silly," he said, leading her back to the train. "St. Louis will still be there tomorrow." If he saw the longing in her face, he ignored it.

"All aboard!" the conductor called. Emily and Clay ran up the steps and to their seats. The train lurched, moving them forward down the tracks. The jarring of the train upset some of the passenger's unsecured belongings, including a baby rattle belonging to a woman sitting across the aisle from Clay and Emily. Smartly dressed in black brocade, the woman tried unsuccessfully to quiet a fussy infant. The baby's painful cries reminded Emily of the time Lizzie had colic.

A weak decoction of mullein had worked well to sooth Lizzie's stomach, and Emily wished now she had some to offer. But since she didn't, Emily decided the best she could do was provide support. Recovering the rattle, she delivered it to the young mother. "I think this belongs to you."

"Thank you." The baby wailed, and the mother's smile weakened. "I can't seem to quiet her, no matter what I do. She doesn't want to eat."

"I'm sure it's only colic."

When the woman looked at her quizzically, Emily continued. "George and Lizzie both had colic when they were babies. Maybe I can be of some help."

Emily asked the porter for a glass of water and a small spoon. Remembering the peppermints she'd saved from her lunch the day before, Emily unwrapped one of the candies and dissolved it in the glass. Using the spoon, she coaxed the baby to drink. After several sips, the baby's stomach seemed to relax, and before long the infant was sleeping.

"I am so grateful," the mother said, accepting the glass and spoon from Emily. "Thank you so much for your help."

"I'm just across the aisle if you need anything," Emily said, giving the mother the last of her peppermints.

"Bless you," the young mother said.

When Emily returned to her seat, Clay commented. "Nice job quieting that baby."

"Doesn't take much to keep them happy," Emily said, embarrassed that he noticed. "Something I learned a long time ago." She took a deep breath and tried to relax her shoulders. Calming a baby with colic was one thing. Attending a child raised with Eastern attitudes was quite another. Pushing away the unwelcome doubts that magnified the closer the train moved to Missouri, Emily consoled herself. If she couldn't fulfill her duties as a companion to Betsy, at the very least, she could work as a nursemaid. If she had to.

She closed her eyes and let her head nod. "There is nothing to worry about," she whispered to herself. She'd be fine in St. Louis. She'd be just fine because she had to.

CHAPTER FOURTEEN

"Something will come of this. I hope it mayn't be human gore."
BARNABY RUDGE

THE MONOTONOUS clackity-clack of metal against metal slowed, becoming less insistent as the train crept into Union Station. Unable to sit still, Emily leaned forward and peered out the window. St. Louis spread around her like a giant quilt. Though it had been only a few weeks ago since she ran down that dusty road away from Saw Tooth City, it seemed like years.

What had Clay said? More than 350,000 people lived here. Imagine a city so big! Why, a person could get completely lost there. For a minute Emily panicked. Then she pushed the thought away, too excited to let fear ruin her day.

Stepping from the train, Emily struggled to breathe. The air was thick and hot like the Harmons' laundry room in the middle of August. The sky was hazy, not clear like in the mountains; the smoky atmosphere turned everything the color of baking cocoa. Emily put her hand over her nose to block the smells of coal, sweaty horses, and spoiling garbage. Even before they left the terminal her dress stuck to her back as if adhered there with paste.

Following Clay to the end of the platform, Emily marveled at the many stages and carryalls ready to transport passengers to their destinations. One large open buggy, grander than any Emily had ever seen in Mrs. Harmon's magazines, especially caught her attention. She pretended it was there for her. She could see herself sitting in the smart carriage with her red satin gown spread over the green brocade seat, waving a handkerchief to onlookers as the horses carried her away.

Clay nodded toward the buggy. "Here we are." Emily gaped at the finest carriage in St. Louis. It couldn't possibly be meant for them. But it was. A tall man with a white head of hair pulled the carriage forward and a girl near Lizzie's age waved. "Uncle Clay! Uncle Clay! I've missed you so much." Clutching a dingy toy rabbit, she jumped down and ran toward them. She threw her arms around Clay's neck and smothered him with kisses.

"Little Bit," he laughed. "My, look how much you've grown. And look at Mr. Ears. He hasn't changed at all."

This stopped the child, who straightened her shoulders and beamed. "I'm getting bigger. Soon I'll be big enough to guide the horses all by myself."

"Not if I can help it." Clay picked her up and tossed her into the air like a rag doll. Emily was afraid he would drop her, but the more he romped with the girl, the louder the child giggled. If this was Betsy, Emily thought, a bit disappointed, she was nothing like Little Nell.

"It's good to have you home, sir." The tall man outfitted in full black livery placed their luggage in the carriage. "You've been missed a great deal."

"Yes you have," the child said, trying to catch her breath. "Grandpapa has been just awful while you've been away." At last she seemed to take notice of the newcomer among them and whispered to her uncle, "Who's that?"

"This is Emily," Clay said. "Emily, may I present Miss Betsy Morrison."

Emily held out her hand. "How do—"

The child stepped closer to her uncle. "What are you doing with her?"

Clay smiled. "She's come to be your new companion."

"I don't need a companion," Betsy said. "Send her away."

Full of vinegar, this one, Emily decided. Not at all sweet like Lizzie or fun-loving like George. Emily's smile froze to her face.

Clay nodded to the coachman. "This is Jonathan."

"How do you do, ma'am?" Jonathan said. His dark face made his curly hair look whiter than snow.

Emily had seen dark people before, but they were all miners, come to work the mines near Rocky Bar. Not sure if she should offer her hand, she merely nodded. "Fine, thank you." She noticed the way he scrutinized her, making her feel as though she were a horse or a buggy being offered for sale.

Clay broke the awkward silence by lifting Betsy into the carriage. "Into the buggy, Miss Morrison." Then he turned to assist Emily.

Miss Morrison? Emily pondered the close resemblance. Surely this wasn't his child, his child with Jenny. Whatever had she gotten herself into? *No*, she reminded herself, the child had called him uncle.

Her fears dissolved into excitement when Jonathan nudged the horses forward. As the carriage moved away from the station, Emily wished the people back in Saw Tooth City could see her. Accustomed only to dust and ore cars, they would certainly envy Emily as she rode through town in the fine carriage. She sat taller and smiled.

"This is for you, Little Bit." Clay pulled the wide-brimmed hat from his head and placed in onto Betsy's head. Emily tried to hide her smile. The hat had never fit him properly; it looked better on the child, even if she should be wearing a bonnet.

"She makes a habit of pretending to be anything but a little girl," Clay said, turning his attention back to Betsy. "And today she shall be a cowboy."

"No I won't!" Betsy pulled the hat onto her head. "I'm a cow*girl*. How do I look?" Without waiting for an answer, she jumped up and tapped the driver on the shoulder. "Jonathan, look at me."

"Sit down, young lady." They hit a loose block in the brick-lined road, and Clay grabbed Betsy by the arm and settled her into her seat to keep her from tumbling out of the buggy.

With her hand over her mouth, Emily was shaking. She was sure she had screamed, sure Betsy would be trampled by the horses. She could see that if she was to be responsible for the welfare of this child, she would have to be more attentive. Especially on outings. But right now she was finding that hard to do, trying to watch the busy streets, the new sights, as well as her companions in the carriage. She had never seen anything more exciting, not even the Fourth of July parade in Rocky Bar.

Jonathan guided the buggy away from the busy terminal with Betsy chattering like a magpie. As the horses' hoofs clomped against the red brick and cobblestones, Emily stared at the large houses and the beautiful gardens, and in spite of the child squeezed beside her in the oversized cowboy hat, Emily smiled. No ore smelters. No noisy stamp mills or rowdy miners. Even though the sky was hazy, Emily smiled at the yellow clouds and her new beginning.

"So tell me, Jonathan," Clay said as the driver guided the horses through an intersection, "how is Father?"

Jonathan turned his head to answer. "I'm sad to say he's been in a most foul temper since you've been away, sir."

"Things at the office?"

"I'm afraid so. And he's had his hands full with this one. When you're away the very dickens gets into her."

Clay patted Betsy on the head. "I'm home now and we'll get that taken care of, won't we, young lady?"

Betsy tipped her head and smiled up at him with a bewitching smile, a smile Emily had seen before. Jenny's. Her fingers turned icy as she stared at the child. She didn't know Jenny had a daughter. But there were a lot of things she didn't know about Jenny. Or Clay Morrison either.

Betsy turned her head and grinned. In that moment Emily remembered the picture in Jenny's locket. If she were to check this child's wardrobe, she was sure she would find an exact copy of the dress the little girl had been wearing in the photo.

If surprise hadn't captured her tongue, Emily would have asked Jonathan to stop the carriage and let her off. She couldn't tend a child who belonged to Jenny. She would not run the risk of seeing the actress again, or Kerry Chapman either. She would have to find…

She tried, but she couldn't move, she couldn't speak. Her heart thumped with an uneven tick. St. Louis was so big, where would she go? While she sat beside Betsy—a child who clearly did not need saving like Little Nell—trying to decide what action to take, Jonathan pulled the carriage to a stop before a large brick manor, bigger than the Palace Hotel. Bigger than the train station, with a frosted glass pane boasting the owner's wealth on the front door. Lafayette Manor.

"We're here," Clay said, and Emily looked up, counting the stories, one, two, three. Why, she would never learn her way around in a house so big. It would take her all day to find the library, let alone Betsy. She stumbled from the carriage, not at all sure she shouldn't retreat to the train station and catch the next Iron Horse back to Idaho Territory.

Inside the mansion, Emily stared at the ceiling, which was at least fourteen feet high. The dark walnut-paneled walls smelled of furniture wax and in spite of the large, massive entryway, Emily felt as if a dark, oppressive mine tunnel threatened to topple in on her at any minute. The tall windows were draped with heavy material, and she wanted to fling the windows open and let some light into the dark room to reflect off the floor-to-ceiling mirrors that glistened like polished silver beside the claret wallpaper. It was easy to imagine she had just stepped into Dickens's Statis House. She truly expected to catch a glimpse of Miss Havisham in her faded bridal gown dashing up the stairs at any minute.

"Who is this?" A thin, plain woman with her hair pulled back so tight Emily could see the blue veins at her temples greeted them, teasing Betsy about her hat.

"I'm Jesse James," Betsy said. "See my new hat, Alice?"

"An outlaw, are we? Well, we'll have no bandits eating in my parlor," the woman said, shooing Betsy inside. She straightened her shoulders and turned. "You must be Emily."

"Yes," Emily answered uneasily as the woman, obviously the housekeeper, given her formal stance and austere attire, scrutinized her.

"Mrs. Talbot," the woman said as if reading Emily's thoughts. "Welcome to Lafayette Manor." The stern woman hustled them inside, seeing to hats and canes while Jonathan attended to the luggage.

Following the merry confusion of welcoming Clay home, Mrs. Talbot motioned Emily aside. "Follow me, please. I will show you to your room. You will want to change your clothes before dinner."

Emily looked at Clay for confirmation.

He nodded. "I think you will find your room next to Betsy's adequate."

Emily looked longingly at the large front door. But instead of bolting she turned and followed Mrs. Talbot to the second floor.

"You will have to see to your own needs," Mrs. Talbot snapped. "There is no lady's maid in this house." Then she added almost as if sniffing, "Don't you own a corset?"

Emily's face reddened at the mention of her undergarments. The corset in her satchel belonged to Kerry; she'd had no time or money to purchase one of her own. She wore a slip and a chemise, but that clearly was not good enough for Mrs. Talbot.

They passed a room filled with more books and toys than she had ever seen in Mr. Belden's mercantile back in Saw Tooth City, or even in the stores in Ketchum for that matter. A pink doll house sat in the middle of the floor; a wooden rocking horse as large as a new pony filled the corner near the window.

Mrs. Talbot opened the door to a small but clean room and turned abruptly, leaving Emily to settle in alone. The room was so spotless Emily was sure Mrs. Talbot slept with a copy of *Mrs. Beeton's Book of Household Management* under her pillow. Wondering what she had done to offend the housekeeper, Emily laid her satchel on the bed and closed the door. No use in running now, she thought as she unpacked her things. She wouldn't be there long. Just long enough to repay Clay the money she owed him; just long enough to find a place of her own.

The muscles in her shoulders started to relax. She had plenty of time. Far away in Idaho Territory, Jenny seemed less of a threat than earlier. Who knew how long it would be before she returned to St. Louis, if ever. And by then Emily would be gone.

Emily turned her attention to the room. Hot and close, despite the grand scale of the mansion it was less than half the size of the space she had shared with George and Lizzie. A narrow bed with a thin mattress snuggled against the wall near the only window, opposite a small wardrobe. Two steps and Emily had crossed the room. She peered out the window, tucked like an afterthought under a low dormer. Stooping, she watched Jonathan lead the horses to the carriage house. He looked like an ant, not at all like the giant she'd stood beside downstairs in the entryway.

Welcome to your new home, Emily thought, turning away from the window to assess the tiny room. For all its fineness, for all the bright sunshine and dogwood blooming outside her window, the house felt unfriendly, colder than ice in winter. More like a cage than a fine stately mansion with fourteen-foot ceilings, large parlors with massive fireplaces. Not to mention Jenny's child.

Very well, Emily thought, I can do this. With embarrassment she slipped out of her dress and into the distasteful corset, remembering the disapproving looks she'd garnered from Jonathan and Mrs. Talbot. But when it came to her choice of dresses, neither would do for her work here. Neither one seemed appropriate for dinner. Since she had nothing else to change into, she shook her soiled traveling dress in an effort to freshen it and slipped it up over her head.

It would have to do, she thought making her way back down the stairs. *As will I.* She sighed. It was going to be a very long summer.

CHAPTER FIFTEEN

"There's light enough for what I've got to do."
OLIVER TWIST

EMILY'S HEELS ECHOED against the wooden steps as she followed the narrow stairs down. *I must be lost,* she thought, wondering how one house could have so many doors, so many staircases.

When she reached the bottom, she pushed the door open to find herself in the kitchen. A short, stout woman with a white apron wrapped around her thick body was slicing bread. She looked up when Emily entered.

"You must be Miss Emily." The woman wiped her hands on her apron and stepped forward to greet her. "I'm Mrs. Koch. Jonathan tells me you've been hired as companion to our own Betsy. Lord knows we need more young'uns around this lonely house."

Emily stood tall under the cook's careful scrutiny, hoping she merited approval. The smell of freshly milled flour and a hint of lemon followed wherever the woman went, and now she moved in a circle around Emily as she examined Betsy's new companion. After completing her inspection, Mrs. Koch gave Emily a hug. "You look hale and hardy enough, up to the task. Now off with you." She nodded toward the door. "They'll be expecting you in the parlor. You won't want to keep Mrs. Talbot waiting."

But Emily lingered in the kitchen. Copper pots hung from a rack near an enormous stove, the likes of which she had never seen, not even in magazines. A copper teakettle whistled on the stove while the cook drew water from a hand pump near the sink. Emily gawked like Lizzie at Christmas. Working in this kitchen would be pure pleasure, she thought, recalling the drafty cook shack in Saw Tooth City with no icebox, and the many trips to Beaver Creek for water.

"May I?" Emily asked, nodding toward the pantry door, unwilling to leave the comfort she found in the kitchen.

"You may," the cook answered.

She poked her head into the pantry, overwhelmed by what she saw. The large storage room reminded her of Belden's mercantile, only this was much better. Tins of teas and boxes of spices lined pantry shelves, along with several bags of grains and flour. There were jars of currants and preserves, lemon drops and assorted dried fruit. More food than she had ever seen in one place, let alone in a storage room. She inhaled deeply, enjoying the fragrance of cinnamon, nutmeg, and exotic teas as she would an expensive perfume. Turning too fast, Emily bumped into a pile of freshly laundered aprons, knocking them to the floor. She picked them up, letting her fingers run across the pressed and starched fabric, almost as pleasing as the material in the dresses Kerry had bought her in Idaho Territory.

When Emily thought of Kerry, her face flamed, and she turned away from the pantry, wishing it were as easy to free herself from her memories of him.

"There you are." Mrs. Talbot huffed through the open door. "We have been waiting for you in the parlor. Come along. Now."

Wishing she could stay behind and help the cook, Emily followed the housekeeper into a large room where tea was being served. Clay sat at a table near an older man. Together, they shuffled through a pile of papers. "You've answered none of these?" Clay asked.

"They weren't important," the older man said.

"They are important. This one in particular could cost us the farm." Clay looked up when Emily entered the room. He put the letters away and said, "Father, this is Emily. The girl I wrote you about."

The older man's gray eyes grew dark as he assessed her. She sensed an iciness about him. Hard and sharp as flint, he could have been Ebenezer Scrooge himself. "Another one of your helpless waifs, no doubt," he said. "Worthless as a three of spades."

Emily studied the pattern in the carpet. She was about to protest that she wasn't helpless, when Betsy burst into the room.

"Look at my new hat, Grandpapa. Isn't it the finest you've ever seen?"

"You look ridiculous," he said to Betsy. "Clayton, you spoil her. It's disgraceful."

"Someone has to." Clay pulled Betsy close and gave her a hug. "From now on you won't be so lonely. Now you will have Emily to play with."

Emily could feel Mrs. Talbot's skeptical gaze, hear her quiet but obvious *humph*. Determined to do a good job, Emily sat down her teacup and offered Betsy her hand. "This is such a big house, Betsy. Would you like to show me your room?"

"No." Betsy shook her head.

"I'd love to see the gardens," Emily said. "Would you care to come with me?"

"No." Betsy clung tighter to her uncle.

"I'm afraid she has missed me more than I thought." Clay offered a weak smile. "Betsy, wouldn't you like to show Emily your pony?"

"No." She turned her head into his chest.

"Well, I'd like to see him." Emily started for the door, thinking Betsy would follow. But Betsy didn't budge, and with her legs already in motion, Emily was too embarrassed to stop and turn around. So she kept walking until she found the door that took her outside.

Alone in the garden, Emily clasped her hands to keep the tremors away. She bit her lip in determination, thinking *somehow* she'd have to find a way to win the child's affection, even if Jenny was her mother. Surely somewhere under Betsy's shy protests was a loving heart. All she had to do was find it.

* * *

To celebrate Clay's return, the evening meal was festive. Course after course of delicious food—a sweet spring soup followed by salmon smothered in cream sauce, braised ham, fresh asparagus, potato rolls, and a delicate sponge-cake pudding—was delivered to the table. A table, Mrs. Talbot had already warned, that was available to Emily and Betsy only on special occasions. Most of Emily's meals would be taken in the kitchen with Betsy or alone in her room. She was granted a seat at this table tonight because it was a celebration; she shouldn't get used to such luxury since she was only hired help.

Betsy devoured two potato rolls without touching anything else on her plate, and Emily wondered if she should scold the child into eating her vegetables. Not tonight, she decided. Tonight they were celebrating.

Emily ate sparingly, wishing she had left her corset back in her room, or at least not cinched it so tightly. Mrs. Talbot watched everything Emily put on her plate or into her mouth, many times lifting her head in disapproval until finally Emily put down her fork and waited to be dismissed. Emily noticed that even though the glasses shone brightly in the candlelight and the silverware sparkled like cut glass, the air rustling the dining room curtains was anything but pleasant.

"Excuse us." Clay stood and nodded to his father. "Father, if you will join me for a brandy in the parlor." In the Morrisons' household, Emily guessed, apparently every night men retired with their brandy, just like she had read about in books. She shivered a little, as if someone had forgotten to close a drafty window. She even pinched her wrist to prove that this was not another daydream, but real life. Hers.

Mrs. Talbot left the room while Emily contemplated her new station. Finding herself alone at the table with Betsy, Emily wondered what to do. Since no one had bothered to tell her the house rules, she had to guess at Betsy's bedtime. And since it was still light outside, Emily assumed it was too early to send the child to bed.

Deciding the best way to handle Betsy was to pretend she was dealing with Lizzie, Emily said, "Betsy, shall we find a book to read in the library?"

At first it appeared Betsy would refuse, but then she seemed to change her mind. "It's this way," she said, leading Emily from the dining room.

Of all the rooms she had seen in the house, the library was Emily's favorite. Rows of books reached from floor to ceiling, so many it took her breath away.

Betsy pulled a book from the shelf and settled onto the couch. "Let's read this one."

Thinking she had finally found something they could do together, Emily smiled and sat beside Betsy. She opened the book, prepared to start reading. But the words on the page looked odd; she couldn't read a single one. It took her a minute to realize the words were foreign, written in Latin or French.

"Begin," Betsy said, waiting expectantly.

"Maybe we should try another book," Emily rose to select another.

"I want to read this one," Betsy said. "This is my favorite. Alice reads it to me all the time."

With book in hand, Emily settled beside Betsy. She opened it and stared at the words, trying to speculate at their meaning. But since the pages contained no illustrations, Emily could only guess at what was written.

"Once upon a time," Emily began.

"That's not what it says." Betsy grabbed the book and began to read. "*Contes de ma mère l'oye.*"

As Emily listened to the fluent way the child pronounced the words, she knew it would take more than a book on etiquette to capture this child's respect and affections.

Mrs. Talbot entered the library, closed Betsy's book, and put it away. "Time for bed," she announced. "Run along. I'll be up in a few minutes."

Emily followed the child, but before she could reach the door, the housekeeper put out a hand to stop her. "I would like a word with you," Mrs. Talbot said. She closed the door and motioned to a chair. "Sit down." Her manner was formal, and Emily felt as if she had been caught stealing the family crystal. "I would like to see your letters of recommendation."

"Letters of recommendation?" Emily said. "I—I don't know what you mean."

"Your references. Surely you wouldn't seek employment without providing references." Mrs. Talbot's chin was firm, the color of stone.

"But Mr. Morrison—"

"Young Mr. Morrison can be impetuous and often forgets the importance of protocol. I'd like to see them now, please."

Where was she supposed to get a letter of recommendation, Emily wondered, looking at the books on the shelves, the heavy drapes at the windows, anything but Mrs. Talbot's face. Even if she dared ask, it would take weeks to get a letter from Mrs. Harmon. She couldn't ask Kerry. If those papers were so important, wouldn't Clay have asked to see them?

"I'm afraid I have none to offer."

"Well, then, how do you expect to stay under this roof? How do we know you won't steal the silver the minute our backs are turned?"

"I wouldn't steal." Emily thought back. Did borrowing Bella's hairbrush constitute stealing? She hadn't kept it, just used it.

"How can we know that? We know nothing of your background, your pedigree."

Emily took a deep breath to control her voice. "My parents are dead."

"An orphan," Mrs. Talbot said. "How original."

Emily considered. Professing the merit of orphans like Oliver Twist to this housekeeper would be useless. Mrs. Talbot was nothing like kind old Mrs. Bedwin. "I don't know how original it is," Emily said, "but it's true."

"Are you telling me there is no one I can contact concerning your past, your credentials?"

"No one," Emily said.

"Wherever did he find you, in the streets?"

Emily raised her chin and met Mrs. Talbot's gaze. "In a mining camp."

It was as if Emily had held a match to a bale of straw, filling the room with flames. "I should have known. I should have turned you out the minute I saw you, dressed like that. The last orphan he brought in ran away with the knives sewn into her petticoats." Mrs. Talbot paced the room, stopped, turned and accused Emily. "I suppose you are very good with a needle, too, aren't you?"

Emily didn't dare tell the housekeeper that yes, she did know how to use a needle. Instead she said, "Mrs. Talbot. I am under the impression that Mr. Morrison has already hired me. And since he didn't deem it necessary to see my references, I hope you will follow his generosity. I have tended children before. If after one month you find me unacceptable, I will leave." Emily didn't know where she found all the words for her speech, but it seemed to be sufficient, because Mrs. Talbot had stopped insisting. Now she was leering.

"One month. Don't get comfortable. You won't be here long." Mrs. Talbot swung the door open with a bang. "And in the meantime, I will have my eye on you."

"You won't be disappointed." Emily stepped out of the room, leaving Mrs. Talbot gaping, still holding the door.

CHAPTER SIXTEEN

"It takes all the running you can do, to keep in the same place."
THROUGH THE LOOKING GLASS

PULLING HER FLANNEL nightgown over her head, Emily listened to the unfamiliar noises around her. It seemed to her that Lafayette Manor, with its massive joints creaking and groaning, would never settle into sleep. Safe in her own small room, Emily shivered. She never felt a place so invasive, so unwelcoming. And yet this was to be her home—at least for a while. She'd best get used to the unfamiliar sounds, the suspicious and disagreeable occupants. She walked toward the small window, brushing her hair with long, even strokes as if the rhythmic brushing of her hair would erase the unpleasant business with Mrs. Talbot. Even though Betsy slept only feet away in the adjoining room, Emily felt lost, empty and alone in the oversized mansion. If she were wise, she would leave come morning.

"Not this time, Emily Ann," she scolded as she sat on the edge of her bed. No matter how disagreeable the housekeeper, she steeled her resolve. Mrs. Talbot would not drive her away.

Feeling alone and isolated, Emily let her thoughts drift to Betsy. How awful to grow up in this bleak house without playmates. Her own playground had been the Saw Tooth Mountains and alpine streams. Even though they weren't her blood relations, she'd had Lizzie and George to romp and laugh with. They'd spent hours at the swimming hole, hours fishing and tossing stones into streams, their days filled with so many adventures they didn't have time to be lonely.

However did a child develop her lungs, or a sense of humor, shut away indoors with only books and lessons and old people? True, Betsy could read French fluently, and her toilet was impeccable for one so young. But where were the rosy cheeks and healthy appetite, Emily wondered, remembering the way Betsy picked at her food, eating only the potato rolls. Too agitated to sleep, Emily paced in front of the window, yanking at a tangle in her hair. References. The disagreeable old woman wanted references.

Thinking a book might help calm her, Emily placed the brush on the dresser. Mindful not to wake Betsy, she tiptoed down the stairs toward the kitchen. Even though she was careful, the steps still creaked beneath her feet. Once or twice she looked back to make sure she wasn't being followed.

The kitchen was empty, but Emily could see a light coming from the parlor. Thinking she would slip quietly into the library for a book, she stopped cold in the hallway when she heard angry voices.

"You promised me you would take care of this while I was gone." Clay's voice thundered from behind the parlor door.

"I didn't have time," his father said. "You ran off chasing some wild dream and left me here to manage a business that still hasn't recovered from the loss of one of its principal partners. I can't take care of everything. Besides," the agitation in his voice subsided, "I instructed Randall to see to it."

"Randall! Randall has no authority. He can't represent anyone in a court of law."

"Clayton, why are we arguing about this? The case was dismissed. The matter is moot."

"Not to Mrs. Wilson." Emily heard Clay pounding on a table. "How do you think she is going to support those children now?" He continued. "You lazy blackleg. You'll fight for your crooked old cronies but when it comes to upholding justice for a commoner, you're too busy. Lord knows what else I'll find undone."

"I don't want to discuss this any more tonight." Heavy footsteps approach the closed parlor door.

"Not so fast. We need to talk about Betsy's boarding school."

"I made all the arrangements while you were gone. The matter is settled. I'm going to bed."

Clay's voice rose. "Father."

"Goodnight, Clayton."

A soft sob spilled from the shadows behind her. Emily peered into the darkness. Even in the dim light, Emily could see Betsy's face, and how hard she was trying to mask her distress with contempt.

"Betsy?" Emily offered her hand, but the child darted by Emily and rushed up the stairs.

"Who's there?" The parlor door opened and Clay's father appeared.

Emily turned and stammered. "Emily, sir. I, I, was hoping to have a word with Mr. Morrison." She dared not say she was going for a book. He might not approve. He might even think she was intent only on stealing, like Mrs. Talbot said. She could feel his scornful observation as he eyed her unpinned hair.

"In the parlor," Clay's father said gruffly. He looked at her with disgust, not unlike the way Mrs. Talbot scrutinized her earlier. "Do something with your hair."

Emily's hand went up to her hair and she wished she were Jonah and the floor a big black whale. But she was only Emily, and this man was the master of the house and even more austere than his son. She moved aside, allowing him to pass. He assessed her suspiciously, then turned and strutted up the stairs to his room.

At the parlor door, Emily hesitated. Clay stood before the mantel, glass in hand as he stared into the empty fireplace. She couldn't see his face but she could feel his anger. Tension hung in the room, heavy and dark like the velvet curtains. Emily took a step backwards, frozen in place. She'd never seen his eyes so black or angry. At first he didn't seem to recognize her. When he looked at her, it was as though he could see straight through her, as if she were a shadow or a ghost. He made a sound like a small laugh and put his glass on the mantel. "Emily," he said as if trying to place her. "What is it?" His voice sounded tired, on the verge of collapse.

Emily backed away. "I, I..." The anger in his eyes frightened her. She opened her mouth but couldn't speak.

"What is it?"

"Mrs. Talbot," she sputtered. "She said I can't stay here without references. She, she wants me to leave."

"She does, does she?" He gave a small laugh. "You are not accountable to Mrs. Talbot. You're accountable to me. I will have a word with Mrs. Talbot before I retire." He tossed what was left of his drink into his mouth. "Anything else?"

"No, sir." She backed out of the parlor. "Goodnight."

Emily ran up the stairs to her room but before she retired, she checked in on Betsy, who was now tucked in her bed with her eyes closed tight. "Sleep tight," Emily whispered, smiling at the way the child squeezed her eyes, careful not to move an eyelash when Emily touched her. She remembered how Lizzie used to reach up and hug her goodnight, and she wondered if this child ever would.

What have I gotten myself into, Emily wondered, not for the first time since she began her journey. Unable to sleep, Emily re-lit the lamp near her bed. She pulled back the mattress and cradled the tin box she had hidden. Settling near the lamp, Emily lifted the lid, let her fingers run across the face of the brooch, and pondered the woman who had once worn it. Hearing a step outside her door, she closed the box quickly and hid it under her mattress—knowing there were some things Mrs. Talbot must never discover.

* * *

The sky outside her window was as hazy as Emily felt. She watched a robin struggle in the humid air, flitting restlessly from tree to tree with a beak full of twigs. She could feel the bird's frustration, its restlessness as it searched for a new home.

Turning from the window, Emily peered into Betsy's bedroom. Having left the door open during the night, Emily knew the child slept little, crying a long time before she fell asleep. And when she did, her rest was troubled. Betsy called for her uncle several times before her breathing evened out and she finally slept. Now, as Emily checked in on her, Betsy rested peacefully, like Lizzie after a hard day at play. *Still early, little one,* Emily thought, tucking the blanket around Betsy. *Sleep.* Standing by the bed watching Betsy, Emily saw more clearly Jenny's delicate features, the color of her hair—and Clay's chin, which looked softer on the child.

She was halfway down the stairs. If this child was Clay's, why didn't Betsy call him Papa? Emily struggled with the image of Jenny and Clay together, then pushed it aside, seeing all too clearly Jenny with Kerry. She shuddered. How long would the image of them together continue to haunt her? All her life, she supposed. Just like the scar on her leg she got as a child when she fell from a tree.

* * *

She was in the library seeking a definition to the word "companion" when Clay appeared.

"Emily," he said. "Good morning."

She almost dropped the dictionary. "Good morning." She turned away to hide the book.

"It seems too early for studies." He took the tome from her and put it back on the shelf. "Join me for breakfast. We need to discuss your station."

In the parlor, over a cup of tea, he continued. "Your duties are quite simple. You're to keep Betsy company. She has become lonely, growing up in Lafayette Manor surrounded by adults."

Emily sipped her tea and watched the casual way he buttered his toast. The wild look she'd seen in his eyes the night before was gone, replaced now with tenderness and concern, surely a father's love when he spoke of Betsy.

"My father would like to send her to boarding school, but she still misses her father, and I'm reluctant to send her off like she's extra baggage one could put into storage." He set his cup down. "Besides, she doesn't want to go, and I would miss her."

Emily didn't know what to make of this confession, and listened intently while he continued.

"I don't expect you to tutor her, but I do expect you to entertain her. Perhaps you ride? Betsy has a pony. We could get one for you. By the way," he added, "I have spoken with Mrs. Talbot. You may find her manners harsh, but she means well."

His speech sounded like a bunch of mumble jumble and polite words, Emily thought. Did that mean she still had to furnish references before she would be allowed to stay? If so, she'd better start packing now. References. Where would she get references? She let her thoughts wander, startling and looking up when she heard him say, "I hope you will be with us a good long time."

"Thank you." She would leave as soon as she could make other arrangements.

"Now, as to your salary. A dollar a day with room and board. With Sundays off."

A dollar a day? Her mouth fell open; he must be mistaken. Never before had she earned so much money with so little effort. At a dollar a day, she calculated, in no time at all she would be able to repay him for her coach and train fare. In less than two months she would be free with a few extra dollars in her pocket.

"Is that acceptable?"

"Yes, sir," she nodded. "It truly is." Standing and waiting to be dismissed, she was already counting the money.

* * *

During her first week in St. Louis, Emily was too busy settling in to her duties to explore the great city. In her spare moments she had taken time to study the directory in the library that showed where to find the river and the names of the streets. On one occasion she accompanied Clay and Betsy into town for yard goods and a stop at a specialty store offering confections and sweets. From the carriage, she tried to pay close attention, craning her neck to watch the street signs, the best way to get about. But with only one trip, she couldn't grasp a clear layout of the city. So with every spare minute, Emily was busy with pencil and paper, carefully copying the map she found in the directory. She kept her ears open, listening to the servants discuss various businesses, writing down names of proprietors she thought might be in need of an extra pair of hands, someone willing to sit hours with thread and needle. She even tucked away an advertisement from an old newspaper she discovered in the bottom of her dresser drawer announcing a clothing factory on Green Street in need of a seamstress. She was hopeful that by finding employment close to the river, she would learn more about the riverboats, perhaps even secure a position with one of the owners. She wouldn't have to sing—she didn't even want to anymore—but she certainly could wash dishes, sweep floors, and make beds.

Emily's chance to explore the city came two weeks later. Sundays were at her disposal, Clay had said. She could accompany the family to church and on to a nice dinner at the Planter Hotel, or she could entertain herself at Lafayette Manor, however she chose. Hoping to set a good example, Emily agreed to accompany the family to church the first two Sundays, but finding the formal dinners at the hotel taxing and her clothes inadequate, she had decided to stay home, claiming personal matters like mending needed her attention.

On this Sunday morning, however, she was so excited she could hardly eat her breakfast. She counted the minutes. It seemed to take the family forever to leave. As soon as they did, Emily put her copied map into her pocket, adjusted her bonnet, and slipped down the back stairs to the kitchen. Looking both ways to make sure no one saw her, Emily was halfway out the door when Mrs. Koch stopped her.

"Where are you off to, Miss Emily?"

"I, I was feeling restless. I thought a walk would settle my nerves."

"A walk will do you good," the cook said. "You've been cooped up in this house all week." Wrapping a small loaf of bread in brown paper, she tucked it into Emily's pocket. "Take care not to get yourself lost. Don't wander too far. St. Louis is no mining camp."

So Emily thought, allowing the cook to straighten her bonnet. They had been talking about her behind her back. *Well, let them. They can talk all they want. They are nothing but a bunch of old biddies anyway, with nothing better to do than gossip.* "I will." She closed the door and slid her hand into her pocket to make sure she still had her map. Without once looking back, she started walking.

She had studied the map long enough to know she would find the river if she headed east. Once she located the river, it was only a matter of following it until it took her to Green Street. She knew if she passed the dry docks, she'd gone too far. Armed with this knowledge, Emily circled the block until she found Park Avenue. It unsettled her a little that the block seemed a mile long. With the heavy humidity in the air, her clothes stuck to her back. But she didn't have time to fret over long blocks and unpleasant weather. Wishing she had a parasol like the one she'd seen months ago in Mrs. Harmon's magazine, Emily held her hand up to block the sun and began to follow Park Avenue.

As she continued down the road, she tried to keep to herself, always looking down or averting her eyes when someone passed on the street. She was painfully aware that she should not be out without an escort, but she had no choice.

Because it was Sunday and the streets were full of carriages, she had to be careful where she stepped. She swatted the horseflies buzzing around her while she wiped her damp forehead. She walked for blocks. She walked for miles. She shook her head "no" when an officer asked if she was lost, obviously suspicious that she had taken to the streets alone. "I hope you are near your destination," he scolded. "A young woman could run up against trouble out and alone on the streets, even if it is the middle of the afternoon. Where is your chaperon?"

"I'm running an errand for my employer," she lied, thinking she wouldn't need a chaperon if she were back in Saw Tooth City.

"Finish your business quickly and return to your employer," he scolded.

"I will."

She knew he was still watching as she turned the corner. She walked a little further, ready to give up and turn back, when she saw the railroad tracks. The river lay just beyond! She ignored her tired feet, the officer's warnings, and her growing thirst as she hurried forward.

Wishing she owned a pocket watch, Emily could only guess at the time. Always quick on her feet, she estimated she had been walking an hour, maybe two, since leaving home. The river had to be near.

And suddenly, there it was, spread out before her like an immense plain. The mighty Mississippi. She clapped her hands like Lizzie would and gazed at the steamboats drifting by, churning the water a dull, muddy gray. The riverboats were much bigger than they appeared in the magazines. Noisy, too, filling the air with a moist sooty grit that clung to her clothes and speckled her hair. The steamboat's whistle sang out loudly, and she jumped. But she thrilled to imagine how much fun she and Betsy could have floating down the river on one of those boats. Perhaps she would suggest an outing to Clay. Betsy was forever talking about riverboats. And Emily understood why. If she had all day, she would like nothing better than to stand there and watch the boats navigate the river, or to wave merrily to the passengers waving back at her from the deck.

For now she couldn't linger. Checking her map, she began walking north, toward Green Street.

She counted twenty blocks, some long, some not so long, but most of them dirty, littered with empty boxes and broken railroad ties. For the most part she ran, trying to follow the riverboats, trying to keep the passengers in sight. Trying to keep as far away from the workmen she saw hovering near the tracks and docks.

It had been several blocks since she'd passed the train turnaround, and once again in the vicinity of streets named Poplar and Almond, Emily slowed her step to ease the pain hitching her side. Spotting an empty bench overlooking the river, she sat down and unwrapped Mrs. Koch's bread. It was crushed and made her thirsty, but she ate it just the same, wishing for a glass of water. Better yet, a glass of lemonade.

She was brushing breadcrumbs from her skirt when a gentleman approached.

"Good afternoon." He tipped his hat with a smile. "You wouldn't be looking for a profitable way to spend your afternoon, would you?"

She had seen men like him before, back in the mining camps. But they didn't try to camouflage their intentions behind a fine suit jacket and top hat. Instead they'd offer gold dust or nuggets and nod their head toward the boarding house or alley. That was, in fact, the very way her mother got her name, according to the rumors. A good amount of gold dust for an entertaining afternoon. "I beg your pardon." She straightened her back and looked him in the eye. "My business is not your pleasure. In fact, how I spend my afternoon is no business of yours at all!" She bustled past him, sweeping his hat from his hand with a swish of her dress. Before he had a chance to protest or retrieve his hat, she was gone.

Deciding that following the river was no longer a good idea, Emily turned down Elm Street and walked a few blocks, knowing once she reached Green Street, she would have to turn back toward the levee. For a while she was content to walk the added distance. Though her surroundings there were not much better, she felt safer. At least there were no unsavory men lurking about, proffering unsavory invitations.

Having memorized the map, Emily knew she couldn't be more than five or six blocks from her destination. The bottom of her feet ached and her hair clung to her face. It never occurred to her that what looked like a mile or two on the directory in the Morrison library could in all actuality be miles and miles of bad roads, putrid odors, and lonely men.

By the way the sun promised to set in the horizon, she knew it was getting late. Later than she had hoped. She had been foolish. She should turn back. But even if she were to turn back now, she would never be able to reach the manor in time for dinner.

With a hard long look toward the setting sun, Emily continued. She'd come this far. According to the ad, she only had two more blocks to go.

CHAPTER SEVENTEEN

Prince Certainpersonio was sitting by himself, eating barley-sugar, and waiting to be ninety. When he saw the peacocks, followed by the carriage, coming in at the window, it immediately occurred to him that something uncommon was going to happen.

HOLIDAY ROMANCE

BY THE TIME SHE REACHED Washington Street, Emily no longer felt safe. Most of the buildings—what was left of them—were vacant. Many were run-down, having had windows and doors shattered or removed years ago. Some were boarded shut with signs posted KEEP OUT. A few were charred, lingering evidence of a great fire. No map could convey the nature of a quarter like this. She took a deep breath to push away the nagging doubts. One more block. One more block and she'd be there.

She passed from Washington onto Green Street, realizing that it had been some time since she saw anyone moving about. In that run-down part of town, she saw no people, no carriages. Only rubbish, debris, and empty houses.

Examining the addresses on the buildings when she could find them, Emily realized she had gone too far. Already in the 400 block, she knew she must turn back toward the river. One block, two.

There! Seeing a large brick building on the corner of a vacant lot, her pulse raced. There it was, 213 Green Street. She checked the ad in her pocket to be sure. She crossed the street and listened for some kind of movement, some noise from the occupants within. But all she could hear was the sound of the trains, the noise of whistles. A rat skittering through the garbage. She walked around the building twice before she saw the address, stenciled in faint black paint on the front door, 189 Green Street.

Emily turned and looked to her left. Where was 213? She ran up and down the block, all the while telling herself she would find it. But as she searched, she realized there was no 213 Green Street. The only building standing was the vacant store on the corner. There were no other buildings, not one person near to answer her questions.

She walked in circles as the sky grew inky. Reluctant to abandon her search but knowing she was out of time, Emily crunched her map into a ball and hurled it at the empty building. With one last glance around the neighborhood, she turned and made her way back to Lafayette Manor, knowing she would have a hard time explaining where she had been and what had kept her away so long.

Tired, hungry, and exhausted, Emily approached the manor with caution, finding only one light burning in the kitchen. Hoping they would all be in bed, she tried the kitchen door, relieved to find it still unlocked. She eased it open. But her relief was temporary; a dark silhouette hovered only inches away. Sure that Mrs. Talbot had waited up for her, Emily took a deep breath and prepared herself for a scolding.

"Get in here, child, before I take a stick to you meself. Running off like that and worrying the very devil out of me."

Happy to find Mrs. Koch instead of the housekeeper, Emily rushed to hug the old woman, only to be held at arm's length. "And where have you been? Do you have any idea what time it is?"

The anger she heard in the cook's voice brought the tears Emily tried all day to hold in.

"Hush it up," Mrs. Koch said, mopping at Emily's face as she would a two-year–old's. "There's warm water on the stove. Wash your face while I make you some tea. And, if you ever pull another prank like this one, I'll tell Mrs. Talbot meself. She'll have you packing faster than you can say please."

Emily had just finished her tea and started up the back stairs to her room when she heard voices.

"Whatever are you doing, making all that noise out here in the kitchen?" Emily recognized immediately Mrs. Talbot's terse tone.

"Trying to get an early start on breakfast, ma'am."

"Nonsense. Off to bed. If you're waiting up for that stray from the mining camps, you can save yourself the trouble."

"Oh, no, ma'am. Emily came in hours ago."

"Are you sure? I didn't see her."

"Yes, ma'am."

Emily sank silently to the stairs and unlaced her shoes, careful not to make a sound.

"Did she say how she spent her day?"

"No, ma'am. I didn't ask. Didn't figure it was any of my business."

Emily sensed awkwardness in the silence. "Turn this light out and get to bed. There's time enough in the morning to see to breakfast," Mrs. Talbot said.

"Yes, ma'am."

Emily waited until the kitchen was quiet before she crept up the stairs to her room. "Thank you," she whispered in the darkness, knowing she'd have to find a way to repay the cook for her kindness and discretion.

* * *

For days, dark thunderclouds threatened. Rain would be welcome, Emily thought, still unaccustomed to St. Louis's unrelenting humidity. Many evenings, when the oppressive heat drove her into the gardens, she reminisced about Saw Tooth City, knowing it would be cool in the mountains, even if during the day temperatures sweltered. As least at night, there would be a moment of relief.

But not here, not in the suffocating heat where for days now the sky had rumbled, pushing tempers into fevers. It didn't surprise her at all when the clouds finally split, spilling over the city. She even welcomed the rain, noting the only drawback was that now she and Betsy were penned indoors.

With each additional day of confinement, Betsy grew more and more restless. More and more irritable, especially with Clay away on another business trip. "When will he be back?" the child said, pressing her nose against the window and watching the storm.

"It may be as long as ten more days," Emily said, pulling the thread taut in her piece of stitchery. "Come, Betsy. If we set our minds to it, we can finish this sampler before your uncle returns."

Like Betsy, Emily wished for Clay's presence. Even though Lafayette Manor was filled with servants, the house felt empty without him. She noticed a marked change in Betsy and the house whenever he was gone, even for a short time. Whenever he left it was as though he was taking away the only sun allowed to shine inside the house, leaving behind gloomy ceilings darker and danker than a thousand mine tunnels.

Dropping the curtain that obstructed her view of the street and the rain that had drizzled relentlessly for two weeks, Betsy joined Emily on the settee. She picked up her sampler but fidgeted after a few stitches. "I want to go outside. I want to see the steamboats."

"Don't be silly," Emily said. "Even if we could persuade Jonathan to take us to the river, there would be nothing to see but rain."

She herself had suggested an outing earlier when she was restless and puttering in the kitchen. But Mrs. Koch was quick to stop her. "Child, don't you give it another thought. Not with thunder and lightning crackling over yer head. A trip outdoors on a day like this is nothing but madness."

Emily sympathized when Betsy sighed. She would love to be free of the house for a while. But even if they did venture to the river, the outing would not brighten Betsy's day. And according to Mrs. Koch, they would be putting themselves in danger. And Emily, from her own secret experience, had to agree.

Later in the day they did get a change in weather. Though thunderclouds still cluttered the sky, the sun broke through, evaporating some of the gloom that drove Emily to the library and Betsy to her room. Eager for fresh air, Emily donned her bonnet and in spite of the occasional falling raindrop, picked her way among the flowers in the garden, leaning over now and then to inhale the damp, clean fragrance. She was enjoying the sweet bouquet of a rosebush when she heard a rattle coming from the carriage house. Betsy was struggling to pull a wagon from the shed. "Can I help?" Emily offered.

"I can do it." Betsy yanked on the red wagon. Caught on a rake, it gave a lurch, and Betsy tumbled to the ground.

"Here." Emily helped Betsy up and brushed the dirt from her dress. "Let's see what's wrong." Emily examined the cart. "Looks like we have a broken wheel here. Bet we can fix it." She slipped into the shed and returned with a mallet. She hammered at the bent wheel, straightening it a bit. She gave the wagon a pull. Though the back wheel wobbled, it worked.

"Guess that's the best we can do." Emily turned to Betsy. But when she looked up, she discovered Betsy was gone, leaving Emily alone in the yard.

"Thank you very much for helping me," Emily said to the empty air, pretending to be Betsy.

"You're more than welcome," Emily replied, brushing the dirt from her hands. She returned the mallet to the shed and walked toward the house, wondering if she and Betsy would ever be friends.

* * *

"Time for lunch," Emily said when she found Betsy upstairs huddled in her bed with Mr. Ears.

"I'm not hungry."

Emily put her hand on Betsy's forehead. "You don't feel too warm," she said. "Do you want me to bring you a tray?"

"I'm not hungry!" Betsy scrunched under the covers. "I'm going to sleep."

"Very well. I'll check in on you later." Emily closed the door, knowing sometimes everyone needed a little quietude.

Later, after Emily finished eating and still believing Betsy asleep, she wandered up to the ballroom. From there she could see the entire city of St. Louis; it spread for miles around her in every direction. Gray clouds massed on the horizon, another approaching storm. Resting her elbows on the windowsill, Emily looked out the window and wondered if somewhere in this big wide city she could find a place to call home.

A movement near the carriage house caught her attention. Emily leaned forward. A tiny figure struggled to lift a small trunk into a red wagon, then tugged the laden wagon out of the yard and down the street.

Betsy? Emily ran down a flight of stairs and pushed the child's bedroom door open. The bed was empty; Betsy was gone. And so was Mr. Ears.

Emily dashed down the stairs and through the kitchen, stopping only long enough to grab a couple of Mrs. Koch's potato rolls, which she wrapped in a clean dishtowel and dropped into her pocket. Outside she ran up the street in the direction she thought she saw Betsy heading. At the corner she looked right, then left. The child had vanished.

Stooping, Emily studied the road. In the dirt she could see what might be tracks from the wagon. Remembering that the back wheel was bent, Emily studied the trail. Yes, there was a distinctive mark in the dirt, a wobbly rut on the left side. She followed the tracks. Her feet were hot in her tightly laced shoes, and she wished she had taken time to discard her corset. Proper attire as it might be, it constricted her chest, making it hard for her to breathe and inhibiting her speed.

For blocks, Emily searched with no sign of Betsy. The farther she walked, the more she remembered her own unsuccessful venture to Green Street, how uneasy she had been walking the streets alone.

Betsy, she thought. *Oh, Betsy, if anything happened . . .*

Overhead, thunderclouds darkened the sky, and a few drops of rain began to fall. Within minutes, rain poured down, soaking into Emily's skin and blurring her eyes. With rain spilling around her and obliterating the last of the wagon tracks, Emily turned back toward the house. She must report Betsy as missing even though they would hold her accountable, even dismiss her for being so irresponsible and losing the child in the rain, for allowing her to venture outdoors in such disagreeable weather. Mindless of her rain-soaked dress and shoes, Emily tried to remember her way back to the manor. Without her map, she was lost.

She was sloshing down a muddy alley when she saw the wagon abandoned in the middle of the road. "Betsy?" Emily called into the storm. Lightning flashed. Behind her, a large wooden crate crashed to the ground.

"Betsy!" Emily searched the alley, looking under every bush, every box, until she discovered the terrified child huddled in a corner under an awning, clutching her soaked gray rabbit. "Are you all right?"

Her clothes covered with mud, Betsy offered no answer. Emily was so glad to have found her, she wanted to hug her, but the child retreated farther into the shadows.

"Look at you," Emily coaxed. "You're soaked to the bone."

"So are you," Betsy finally said with a sniff, and allowed Emily to come closer.

Emily wiped the mud from Betsy's dress the best she could. Then she held the child close to stop her shivers. "Where were you going?" When she got no answer, Emily hunched down until she was almost sitting on the ground, level with Betsy. She opened her dishtowel to remove the potato rolls. But they, too, were soaked and fell apart when Emily unwrapped them. Able to save only one small piece, Emily gave this to Betsy, who devoured it in one hungry bite.

"I was just about your age the first time I ran away from home," Emily said with a nod.

Betsy tipped her head and looked at Emily. "I'm never going back."

"Where will you go?"

Betsy squared her shoulders and set her chin. "To see the steamboats."

Ah, the steamboats. She should have known. "How exciting," Emily said. "I love steamboats."

Betsy cocked her head. "You do?"

"Of course. I used to spend days and days staring at their pictures in all the magazines. Until Mrs. Harmon would thump me on the head and tell me to get on with my work." She imitated Mrs. Harmon, which made Betsy laugh.

As quickly as the rain had appeared, it stopped. When the sun returned, Emily stood and extended her hand to Betsy. "Well, Miss Morrison. It has been a pleasure. Thank you for sharing your fine company with me. Now I must go."

"Where are you going?"

"Oh, you know." Emily pointed to the rainbow streaking the sky. "To find that pot of gold."

"What pot of gold?"

"The one at the end of every rainbow."

Betsy looked toward the sky with suspicion. "Do you think it's really there?"

Emily nodded, all seriousness. "I most certainly do."

Betsy's suspicion turned into curiosity. "Is it far?"

"I'm not sure," Emily said. "Would you like to help me find it?"

"What about the steamboats?"

"The steamboats will be there long after the rainbow disappears. We can see them later, after we find the pot of gold. Shall we?"

Betsy thought about this a moment. "Yes."

"Well, then, Miss Morrison. We best be on our way. It can be a very long journey."

After wringing the water from Mr. Ears, Emily drained the wagon. She extended her hand to Betsy, who hesitated briefly as if considering her options. Several moments passed before Betsy curled her fingers around Emily's, and together they vacated the alley and walked down the muddy street, pulling the wagon.

As Emily led Betsy toward the rainbow, she tried to decide. Now that she had the child's confidence, could she persuade her to return home? They walked for a while until Betsy complained. "My feet hurt." She limped, lagging behind Emily and the lopsided wagon.

"I'm tired of looking for gold." Betsy sat down on the rickety wooden boardwalk, her once springy curls limp and sticky with rain and humidity. "And I'm hungry."

So am I, Emily wanted to say, but instead she encouraged, "We're almost there. Look, I'd wager it's just around that corner." Struggling to keep their spirits up, Emily refused to give into the fear gnawing inside her like hunger pains. Betsy hadn't caught on but it was very apparent to Emily that they had wandered into a district filled with warehouses. They were lost, and by Emily's calculations a long way from home. By the look of the surrounding neighborhood she had led Betsy into a very undesirable part of town, not unlike Green Street. Taking a deep breath to calm her fears, Emily rubbed her nose. What was that awful smell? Fish?

Rotten fish. And foul-smelling water. She looked again. Yes, water. Through the small space between the two abandoned buildings across the street she could see it shimmer. She could even hear it lapping against the dock. A whistle blew in the distance. *The train.* If only she had led Betsy toward the train station instead, there would be people there to help her. Someone she could ask for directions.

A bird cawed and she looked up to see a seagull perched nearby on a broken post. Disheartened, she turned to see Betsy's face glowing.

"Look," Betsy pointed. "Look, Emily. We found the river." Betsy was so excited she clapped her hands and for a minute reminded Emily of Lizzie.

"I think I see a steamboat. Hurry!" Betsy ran toward the river. "Look. Over there. It's Bloody Island."

Unwilling to leave the wagon behind, Emily pulled the lopsided wagon, trying to keep up with Betsy. "Betsy, please slow down. *Wait.* Wait for me!"

Emily tripped on her dress, tearing the hem, and had to stop. "Betsy?" Emily rounded the corner in the growing dusk and peered into the night air. "Betsy, where are you?"

She cupped her hands to her face and called. "Betsy? Betsy?" The wind carried her voice out over the water along with the cries of a lonely seagull. Forgetting the wagon, Emily ran to the wharf, calling again. "Betsy? Betsy? Answer me!" But the only thing she heard was the sound of water as the waves of the Mississippi River crashed into the shore.

CHAPTER EIGHTEEN

He was sailing over a boundless expanse of sea, with a blood-red sky above, and the angry waters, lashed into fury beneath, boiling and eddying up on every side.
THE PICKWICK PAPERS

FARTHER DOWN THE BANK, Emily saw Betsy jumping up and down and waving to a paddleboat.

"Careful!" Emily rushed forward, agitated but relieved. She reached out a hand to grab the child back from the river's edge. But at the sound of Emily's voice, Betsy turned, slipped, and fell into the water.

"Betsy!" Emily didn't even have to think, but immediately dove into the Mississippi River. She swam as hard as she could but she underestimated the power of the current, and her wet clothes slowed her down. This was like no stream back home in Idaho Territory. By the time she reached Betsy, her arms ached. Her fingers felt like rubber.

"Grab on to my neck," she told Betsy, as they both treaded water. With one arm around Betsy and trying to stay afloat, Emily looked to the shore and then at the paddleboat. She would never have enough strength to make it back to shore. She looked at the boat again. It wasn't too far away. If only she could raise someone's attention. "Help!" she screamed. "Somebody, help us!"

Betsy clung to Emily's neck. Sputtering and coughing, it was all Emily could do to keep Betsy's head above water. She saw a deckhand near the side of the boat and yelled at him, "Help—over here!"

The closer they got to the boat, the choppier the water became. Emily was near enough to touch his hand when a large wave crashed over their heads. Gulping muddy water, with arms aching,

Emily pushed Betsy forward, toward the man. She could feel her body lighten as he lifted Betsy up over the side of the boat. She was waiting for him to reach down for her when the current pulled her under, closer to the hull, close enough she could see the rotating paddle. She thrashed in terror under the churning water. She felt a thud followed by a sharp pain. Her head felt as though it had exploded. Her arms began a lazy crawl as she sank below the water's surface. As she dropped further, she watched her world turn gray, then black.

* * *

"Betsy!" Emily tried to scream, pushing at the branches holding her down, under the water. Determined, Emily struggled and kicked until she set herself free.

"Call for the doctor. I think she's waking." She could hear Kerry talking and she wondered what he was doing there in the river. "Kerry?" Emily said. "Help me."

"I'm here, Emily. I'm right here."

She reached her hand out to Kerry, eager for his touch. But when she opened her eyes, Emily found that she was no longer in the river. She was in a room she had never seen before and it was Clay, not Kerry, leaning over her, his face furrowed with concern.

"Hello, there, Miss McIntyre," his face relaxed a little when her eyes focused. She tried to sit up, but the pain in her head pushed her back against the pillow.

"You gave us quite a scare," Clay said.

"Betsy," Emily said. "Where's Betsy?"

"Here I am. And Mr. Ears too. We're taking care of you along with Mrs. Foster."

Emily reached out her hand. "Little Bit," Emily whispered. Hugging the stuffed rabbit, she slipped into a long dark sleep.

Often it was a troubled sleep, and she would wake never sure of where she was or what she was seeing. Once she dreamt she was splashing in Beaver Creek with Lizzie. Rain was pelting so hard against the window she was sure she was drowning all over again.

Another time, Betsy was perched on the side of Emily's bed playing with a treasure chest of jewels. Necklaces dangled around her neck; bracelets adorned each wrist. "And this," Betsy was saying," is the very best of all. Grandmother's ring." The large ruby ring sparkled as Betsy slipped it on her finger and flashed her hand. "Don't you agree?"

When Emily truly woke, many weeks later, she was disoriented, believing again she was still in the river. "Betsy," Emily called. "Betsy?"

"Sshh," Clay said, "Betsy's safe."

"The river," Emily coughed. "She went into the river." Although her mouth was dry, it tasted awful, like muddy water. Her head hurt; her arms and legs felt like thin soggy noodles. Her chest ached when she coughed.

There was a knock at the door and Clay looked up. "Good," he said, "the doctor is here." He held her hand for a moment, then squeezed it for reassurance. "I'll be right outside if you need me."

Using a strange instrument he called a stethoscope, the doctor listened to Emily's lungs. It was cold against her skin and made her shiver. "Sit up," he instructed. He looked into her eyes and checked her reflexes. "You are one lucky lady," the doctor said when he finished his examination. "We almost lost you."

No wonder her body felt so tired, as if she had just crawled out from under an ore car. She lay back against her pillow, confused and exhausted.

"I want you to stay in bed. We can't have you catching bronchitis as well as pneumonia." The doctor tucked the quilt up under her chin. "And do as Mrs. Foster tells you, hear now?"

"Mrs. Foster?" Emily looked around the room, but they were alone. The curtains were open allowing the sun to fill the room with hope and fresh air. She wanted to stay awake and enjoy the sunshine, but her eyes were heavy, her body begged for sleep. She wanted to ask how long she'd been ill, but the doctor had already packed his black bag and headed for the door, where he stopped to confer with Clay. She couldn't hear what they said, but the look on Clay's face told her it wasn't good.

When the doctor left, Clay pulled a chair close to the bed. She noticed a bouquet of daises behind him on the table. "How do you feel?" he asked.

"Better."

"Rest. I'll be right here if you need me."

Emily struggled to keep her eyes open. But as they quivered shut, she couldn't stop wishing it was Kerry's face she was seeing, Kerry's voice welcoming her back from the deep.

* * *

Emily was so sick she lost track of time. She wasn't sure if she'd been in bed for one day, one week, or one month. As the days blurred together she wanted only to sleep. When she was lucid, she remembered seeing a woman dressed in a maid's uniform, only white, attending to her needs. Mrs. Foster, they called her. A woman who could've been her mother's age, with hair the color of Bella's spilling from under her white cap.

When Emily thought of Bella, she remembered Kerry, and the pain in her chest was so sharp she gasped for air. Or maybe it was the mustard plaster Mrs. Foster applied to her chest, spoiling the smell of the daisies that always seemed to be freshly picked. "Drink your soup," the nursemaid instructed.

Emily sipped the clear beef broth, but as soon as Mrs. Foster left the room, she removed the offensive remedy from her chest, which she hid under the bed. She turned at a knock on the door.

"Come in." She adjusted her nightdress, hoping it wasn't Mrs. Talbot, who did her best to avoid the sickroom during Emily's illness.

"You're looking better," Clay said, opening the door. When Emily tried to sit up, he settled her back against the pillow. "Not so fast. You need your rest. You took a mighty blow to the head."

"I need to see to Betsy." Now that she was stronger, she had much time to make up for. And surely bills from the doctor and nursemaid to pay. But her head throbbed. She felt woozy when she tried to move.

"You need to get well," Clay said.

"Where am I?" Emily asked, glancing around the room.

"My grandmother's bedroom," Betsy said, poking her head into the room. "No one can come in here."

Until she took ill, it seemed. Emily might have lain abed for many days clutching Betsy's rabbit, but this was the first time Emily really examined the room she occupied. It was cheery, not dark like the rest of the house. With glass doors that opened out to a garden. Emily studied the yellow wallpaper, flecked with faded roses, and remembered how she enjoyed helping Mrs. Harmon hang paper in the new parlor just last fall. Someone loved this room very much, Emily thought, surprised at the unexpected sense of peace she felt there.

"This used to be my mother's room," Clay acknowledged.

"I like it very much." Emily watched the way the curtains wisped at the window. She would like to stay here a good long time.

"I'm glad you didn't die." Betsy pushed closer, reaching for Emily's hand.

"Betsy." Emily leaned forward. "Thank you so much for sharing Mr. Ears with me. He helped me get well." She kissed the tip of the toy's nose and gave the rabbit back to Betsy.

"You're welcome." Betsy hugged the rabbit. "He helps me when I'm sick, too."

They turned at a knock at the door. "How is our patient today?" Emily looked up to see the doctor standing in the doorway.

"Much better," Clay answered for her, shooing Betsy aside.

"Looks like she's getting back her color."

"And her spirit," Clay said. "She thinks she is well enough to get out of bed." Clay and the doctor laughed. They talked about her as if she wasn't there and even though she knew they were all concerned, she was glad when they left, allowing her to rest and enjoy the pleasant room by herself.

Later, when she tried to stand, she was surprised her ankles wouldn't hold her.

"What do you think you are doing?" Mrs. Foster caught her before she toppled to the floor. "Get back in bed," she said sternly.

"Thank you." Snuggled in bed like a caterpillar, Emily closed her eyes. Safe and warm, she drifted off to sleep, hoping she would wake well and worthy.

* * *

"Watch." Betsy pumped her legs so the swing would carry her higher.

"Be careful," Emily called. From where she and Clay sat engaged in a game of checkers, they could watch Betsy as she played outdoors. Clay's mother must have been able to sit just like this, Emily thought, and keep an eye on Clay when he was little.

"I fell out of that tree when I was five and broke my arm," Clay said noticing how Emily's gaze lingered on the large willow. "Father never forgave me."

Emily cocked her head. "Why not?"

Clay's eyes were reflective. "He was determined to make an attorney out of me. I was supposed to be indoors with my books instead of playing in trees." He pushed his dark hair away from his face, and Emily thought how strange he looked at times, so unlike an attorney.

"At five? So young?"

Clay nodded. "My father's first priority is always business."

She tilted her head and observed him. She could smell the warm scent of leather and just a trace of soap, and she wanted to reach up and touch his face. Instead, she turned away, as if getting too close would blister her fingers or send her body into spasms. If she'd learned anything from her attachment to Kerry, it was to be cautious and wary.

Later, after most of the house had retired for the evening, Emily convinced Clay to help her outside, claiming the night air would serve as an elixir. He settled her on a blanket near the willow tree and they contemplated the day as a warm breeze rustled the air around them. Other than the sound of crickets, the evening was quiet, at peace.

"This is nice." Emily leaned back and looked up at the emerging stars. She closed her eyes and inhaled, enjoying the smell of evening and garden roses. Occasionally she whiffed warm leather and soap, and inhaled deeply.

Under the light cast from the window, she watched Clay nibble on a blade of grass. His hair was mussed. He had left his vest and tie inside and rolled the sleeves of his shirt up to his elbows. Lying in the grass, he looked like a boy, like George when he was up to mischief. She could feel her heart open and had to look away.

Insects buzzed near her face, and she swatted at the air. "They're in my hair!" she said, her voice rising. "They'll set it on fire!"

Clay laughed so hard Emily thought he would succumb with laughter. Fireflies," he said, trying to catch his breath. "We call them lightning bugs."

Feeling stupid more because he laughed so hard than because she didn't recognize the insects, Emily said, "They glow."

"They do," Clay nodded. "Tom and I used to make lanterns by trapping them in Mason jars." He showed her how to capture them, how to hold them in her hands. Her fingers tingled, and she wished Lizzie and George were here to see the delightful insects.

He must have known what she was thinking because he mentioned Betsy. "Little Bit likes to catch them like this." He imitated the child, cupping his hands until he had a fistful of bugs.

"She's an affectionate child," Emily said. "She's very fond of you."

"And I'm very fond of her," Clay said, "but sometimes that isn't enough."

Emily remembered her own father and Mr. Harmon. "Sometimes that's all there is."

It was a while before he broke the awkward silence. "I promised Tom I would look after her. Often, I fear, I let him down."

"Tom?"

"My older brother. Betsy's father."

She felt a flood of relief. Finally, she had the truth. He really was Betsy's uncle, and not her father. Emily knew so little about him, she thought, close enough to touch his face. Instead, she turned away. Must be something in the night air, an unknown substance that made one melancholy, longing for something concrete, permanent, and just out of reach.

"We should go in." He adjusted the shawl around her shoulders. "And when you feel better, we can begin our search for your relatives."

"No," she sputtered, trying to stop the caution and fear rising inside her stomach like Mrs. Koch's bread dough. The time had come, and yet if she told Clay the truth—that she had no relatives in St. Louis, or anywhere else for that matter—he would send her back to Saw Tooth City on the morning train without thinking twice. She would never see Betsy, St. Louis, or Clay for that matter, ever again.

"If we don't, you're likely to relapse," he prompted, believing her protests related to time and weather rather than lies and ancestors.

Her smile was weak and guarded as she let him lead her indoors. She tried to push the apprehension away like one did a fly determined to ruin a freshly baked pie cooling on the windowsill. But no matter how hard she tried, the foreboding would not leave her.

CHAPTER NINETEEN

"…tell Wind and Fire where to stop," returned madame;
"but don't tell me."
A TALE OF TWO CITIES

AFTER A TROUBLESOME NIGHT, Emily woke determined to move back into her old room near Betsy, determined to make herself useful, an asset rather than a burden. Dressed and ready for breakfast, she startled Mrs. Talbot in the parlor. "What are you doing in here?" the housekeeper asked, believing they were alone.

Planning to steal your precious silver, Emily would like to have said, but she held her tongue and smiled. "I'm feeling much better. I should like to join the family for breakfast."

"That would be wonderful," Clay said, startling them both when he entered the room. "Tell Mary to set another plate."

"Yes, sir," Mrs. Talbot said with a coldness even the morning sun couldn't penetrate.

"Are you sure you should be out of bed?" Clay said as they settled at the breakfast table.

"She's feeling much better," Mrs. Talbot said, mimicking Emily's earlier declaration.

"I am," Emily nodded, determined to remain unriled. "I'm well enough to be up. And I sent Mrs. Foster home." She saw Mrs. Talbot's eyebrows rise.

"You have all been so kind," Emily continued, pausing only long enough to offer Mary her cup for tea. "And I can't thank you enough for your consideration. I have moved back into my old room and am ready to resume my duties."

"I want you to take caution," Clay said. "We can't have you suffering a relapse."

"I will," Emily said, wondering what to do with the feelings she had for Betsy and Clay growing inside her like a hunger only love could fill. She knew she should be careful, wiser than Alice when tempted to sip from a bottle marked DRINK ME, wise enough to leave this table and family before her heart stopped her, before he discovered who she truly was. Before it was too late.

Later that afternoon, when the house was quiet and Betsy was in the library reading *La Petite Famille* to Mr. Ears, Emily slipped up to her room and retrieved her tin box. What is it, she thought, reaching her hand under the mattress, that drives a mother away from a child? Perhaps the child was unworthy. Emily struggled to understand what drove her mother to the dirty mining camp of Atlanta in Idaho Territory, and Jenny away from Betsy. But the box was not where she had left it. Or had she forgotten, during her illness? She threw back the covers, and lifted up the mattress. Nothing.

Believing Betsy had been up to her tricks again, Emily searched the child's room too, but the tin box was nowhere to be found. In the library, Emily confronted her charge. Knowing Betsy loved to play hide and seek, Emily asked, "There is something missing from my room. Do you suppose you can help me find it?"

"Sure," Betsy set her book aside. "What are we looking for?"

Emily expected Betsy to giggle and give up the ruse, but it was clear from the child's actions that she had no idea what was missing. So, Emily made a game of it, searching the house in pretense, when finally, they ended up back in Emily's room where Emily picked up her pillow and exclaimed, "Ah, there it is!"

"What?" Betsy said, staring at the empty bed.

"My dreams and imagination." Emily tickled Betsy until she squealed.

"Oh, you." Betsy stomped off to play with her rabbit. But later, when Betsy thought she was alone, Emily saw her searching under her own pillow.

Later, that night, before Emily crawled into bed, she looked under the mattress again, expecting to find nothing. But she was surprised. There the box was, almost in the same place she had left it. She checked the contents. Everything was there—the brooch, the picture, and the pennies. Her heart raced. And something else. Something that didn't belong to her.

Emily picked up the ring—the same ruby ring Betsy played with when Emily was ill. Clay's mother's ring. Emily's hand shook.

What was it doing in her room?

She dropped the ring into the box and tucked the box away, this time in a safer place. She'd have to find a way to return the ring before the housekeeper reported it missing.

Emily tried to sleep, but the questions kept circling her head. If Betsy didn't put it there, who did? If Betsy did, why would she lie? And who else knew she was searching for the box? The mystery kept Emily awake as she struggled to find an answer.

* * *

There'd been a stir in the house all week, and Friday morning arrived with excitement. Emily could feel it in the breeze drifting through her open window. She dressed quickly and checked in on Betsy, only to find her up, peering into her closet.

"What's this?" Emily said, entering Betsy's room.

"Bastille Day. We're going to the festival. What shall I wear?"

Having never heard of Bastille Day, Emily could only guess. "This is pretty," she said, helping Betsy look over her dresses, stopping at a pale pink linen.

"That's too small."

"What about this one?" Emily's hand faltered. She was sure she was looking at the same dress the child wore in the picture in Jenny's locket.

"Maybe this will do." Clay stood near the open door with two large boxes tied with ribbon.

"Uncle Clay!" Betsy ran to him with a hug.

"There was so much noise up here I thought we had rats in the rafters." He gave Betsy a hug. "I thought I'd better see for myself." He looked over her head at Emily and smiled.

Emily cautiously returned his smile, wondering what he was up to.

"What's in the boxes?" Betsy said.

"Why don't you open them and find out?" He handed one to Betsy and the other to Emily.

Betsy ripped open her package. Inside, she found a soft white dress. She held it up and Emily could see the delicate lace trim, the pink sash.

"Oh, Uncle Clay. Thank you." Betsy threw her arms around his neck.

He nodded to Emily. "Open yours."

Emily's fingers shook as she tried not to tear the brown paper. Inside, she found a blue and white walking dress, in the latest mode, trimmed with velvet ribbon bows. "It's beautiful." She touched the soft fabric, afraid if she held it up in front of her, it would vanish.

"I had to guess at your size. I hope you like it."

Tears formed in the corners of her eyes. A dress made especially for her. She didn't even think, but stepped forward and, like Betsy, threw her arms around his neck. "Thank you so much."

His face turned red, but he didn't pull away. "You're welcome. Consider it our gift to you for making Betsy so happy."

She looked at the dress and wondered if Mrs. Talbot would approve. "It's much too nice," Emily said. "I can't accept it." She heard the words, wishing she didn't have to say them.

"Nonsense." He winked at Betsy. "It isn't going to fit anyone else in this house." He clapped his hands as if to draw their attention. "Ladies, go try them on." He smiled and Emily noticed the tender look in his eyes, a look that lingered long after he left the room.

Betsy began working the buttons on her nightgown. "Do you need some help?" Emily asked, as Betsy struggled to pull the new dress over her head. Unfastening the buttons so Betsy could slip into it easily, Emily stood back to admire. "Your uncle has excellent taste." She tied Betsy's sash into a big pink bow and said, "There. You look lovely, Miss Morrison."

Betsy giggled, "Now you."

Back in her room, Emily slipped into her corset and petticoat. She adjusted her bustle and tried on the new walking suit. It fit perfectly, transforming her into a more grown-up version of herself than she'd ever imagined. She fought at the tears spurred by his generosity.

Emily studied her reflection in the mirror, running her hands across the soft fabric. Even with her plain face, she looked like a fine lady, like the pictures she'd seen of women shaded by silk parasols watching steamboats in Mrs. Harmon's copy of *Harper's Bazaar*.

Pulling her hair up and securing it with pins, Emily smiled at her reflection. Pretty. Like Jenny. She sneaked one final glimpse of herself in the mirror. No, she decided. Prettier than Jenny.

Betsy skipped down the stairs, pirouetted before her uncle, and asked, "How do I look?"

"Like a princess," Clay smiled. He glanced up when he saw Emily on the stairs, his smile fixed in place. The words slipped from his tongue, and Emily wasn't sure if the compliment was for her or if he still referred to Betsy, but in her new dress she didn't care. With her head high, she descended the stairs, almost as excited about celebrating Bastille Day as Betsy. She couldn't have felt more regal if her birthright was that of a true princess or Queen Victoria herself.

Her excitement was marred only by Mrs. Talbot's stern reprimand when they were alone in the foyer. As Emily collected her bonnet, the housekeeper chided, "No decent woman accepts presents from a man. Unless they are married. And have no doubt, he has better sense than to marry the likes of you."

In spite of the implied threat in the housekeeper's words, Emily tied her bonnet and said, "Excuse me, I can't keep them waiting." She left Mrs. Talbot glowering in the hall while she hurried to join Clay and Betsy. As Clay helped her into the carriage, Emily thought, *nothing will ruin this day*. Nothing. For this one day only she would not brood about her past. She would not worry about being good enough. Nor would she worry about spiteful and troublesome housekeepers.

CHAPTER TWENTY

"Off with her head! Off with— "
ALICE IN WONDERLAND

AS THE CARRIAGE DREW closer to Kuhn's Garden, the excitement in the air was so thick Emily could hold out her hand and touch it. Her fingers tingled the way they did the night she and Clay caught fireflies under the willow tree. While Jonathan saw to parking the carriage, Emily, Clay, and Betsy strolled through the open-air garden, past vendors with wagons of fruit, baked goods, and flowers.

"There must be hundreds of them," Emily said. Pushcarts lined the streets, creating a carnival atmosphere as she watched merchants dressed in gay costumes—some as trappers, some as royalty—peddle their wares.

Clay stopped in front of a cart selling vanilla cakes. "We'll take some of those."

In the distance, Emily could hear a band playing tunes suitable for a military invasion. She was surprised to see men dressed as French soldiers, cravats at their necks, carrying rifles or sabers, marching up and down the streets in step with the music.

As Emily, Clay, and Betsy moved through the crowd, several women dressed much like Emily on the arms of beaus or husbands, sheltered from the sun by lace parasols and straw hats, nodded to Emily with a passing smile. Everywhere they went people stopped to speak with Clay. Emily was surprised at his many acquaintances. They could not turn a corner without running into someone he knew.

Emily held her head higher. She tried to smile properly when introduced, pushing away her feelings of self-consciousness. His friends wouldn't smile so graciously, she thought, if they knew she was just the hired companion. Or even worse, a prostitute's daughter instead of the fine lady she pretended to be.

Before the sun could blister her nose, Clay stopped at a booth and purchased two lace parasols, one for Betsy and one for Emily. Dressed as finely as any other woman in the square, Emily opened her parasol. She couldn't help but notice how passersby looked at her, not with curiosity but with respect and admiration. She couldn't help but compare this outing to her strolls with Kerry in Ketchum. Her face flushed with humiliation as she remembered.

"This way." Clay steered them toward the corner of Sidney and Buel, where a crowd had gathered to watch the parade.

"*Allons enfants de la Patrie, Le jour de gloire est arrivé*!" the people sang, waving tricolored flags with broad stripes of blue, white, and red when the Arsenal Band passed.

"Where are the stars?" Emily said, accepting the small hand flag Clay purchased from a street vendor.

"On the American flags," Clay said, joining the crowd waving his banner. "*Vive la France!*"

"*Vive la France*," Emily echoed, waving her flag along with the others, noticing that indeed there were two flags flying at the celebration. One for America, the other for France.

"Here they come," Betsy shouted.

While Clay held Betsy up so she could see, Emily stood on tiptoe, trying to watch as the parade marched by. This wasn't Emily's first parade; she'd seen parades before. Back in Rocky Bar, where every Fourth there was a tremendous parade with a grand marshal and marching band. All mining ceased as ore cars were decorated with flags and colorful ribbons. The manes and tails of horses and mules would be braided and adorned with flowers and red, white, and blue ribbons as miners and merchants led their animals down Main Street. There were horse races and a greased-pig chase and always a street dance that lasted until sunrise. The grand marshal or town sheriff recited the Declaration of Independence, and everyone sang "America." When it was finally dark enough to light the fireworks, large blasts of dynamite reverberated through the canyon, causing the hastily erected shelters to tremble like leaves on aspen trees. Later, the miners crowded the saloons, where music played long into the night.

Yes, she'd seen parades before, but they were nothing like this. Never so long, with thousands of people waving French and American banners as wagons and pushcarts passed by carrying an array of people in powdered wigs, or women in lavish gowns with yards and yards of silk and brocade, dressed as ladies of the court. Or men outfitted to look like King Louis, and others as French trappers.

"What's that?" Emily whispered when a cart passed filled with melons lopped in half, colored red in places to look like blood.

"The guillotine," Clay said. "The Reign of Terror."

"It's gruesome." Emily turned away so she wouldn't have to watch the cart that followed filled with faux dead bodies.

The parade was long and it was hot standing in the sun, even under her parasol. When the procession finally ended, they strolled through the open-air market, stopping to examine the fresh fruits, flowers, and pastries. Emily knew nothing about the French Revolution except what she had read in Dickens's book of two cities, but she got a full explanation as they passed characters dressed as French soldiers, King Louis XVI, and Marie Antoinette. Admiring the gowns worn by the many impersonators, Emily thought it must have been exciting to have been queen of France until she witnessed later in the day the beheading ceremony of Queen Marie's fate at the guillotine. She had a hard time understanding how Madame Defarge could sit and casually knit as people all around her were losing their heads.

Later, they stopped at a booth selling hats. Clay selected for himself a tricorne that reminded Emily of the one she had seen in pictures of George Washington and was similar to the one King Louis wore in the parade. The bonnet he purchased for Betsy was whimsical, a pert straw with ostrich feathers and ribbons. He settled the hat on Betsy's head, and Emily watched with envy.

"Which would you like?" he asked Emily.

"Oh. I, I…I already have a hat." She looked at her hands, embarrassed, knowing she couldn't afford a new hat.

"Give us that blue silk. The one there with the rows of lace," Clay said.

Before she could protest, he untied her bonnet and set the new hat on her head. "Quite charming, Miss McIntyre," he said. "Quite charming."

First a dress. Then a parasol. And now this? What would the servants say when she returned home with more gifts? Would they think he was taking advantage of her station, perhaps even make fun of her? Or would their tongues wag in whispers, hinting at his intentions toward her?

A month ago she wouldn't have had such thoughts. In the mining camp, when a person gave a gift they were usually sharing their good fortune with others. But here, in polite society, Emily was learning gifts were not the same. Gifts often came with a higher price and consequences.

"Thank you." She wondered herself what his intentions were, what his price would be.

After paying for his purchases, Clay offered her his arm. As they walked among the people, Emily pretended she was Lucie Manette. She replayed Dickens's story in her head, fancying Kerry as Charles Darnay, so self-engrossed he was willing to let another die in his place. She imagined Clay to be Sydney Carton and was proud to be seen on his arm in public.

They passed more people dressed in costumes. Some reminded her of mad Dr. Manette, forever making shoes in the dark Bastille, and it gave her comfort knowing that even though her father was dead, he'd died with honor.

There were so many people around them Emily couldn't watch everything. More often than not she found herself watching the husbands and wives. The families. The mothers tending their children. More than once she thought about the day she watched with longing as the Harmons walked to church, leaving her behind.

Someday, she thought as she strolled with Clay and Betsy, she would have a family of her own. But today she was happy, content enough to pretend.

They crossed a street and Clay stopped abruptly. "This way." He led Emily and Betsy away from a cluster of women. He didn't have to tell her that these women were prostitutes. She could tell by his actions and by the way the women were dressed, exposing their legs and dark silk stockings.

Emily couldn't help but notice how men and women went out of their way to avoid the corner where the women gathered. Or how the prostitutes smiled, hoping to catch the attention of the single men. She could hear the whispers, the crude remarks. But that didn't stop her from looking, searching the empty faces of the fallen women. She focused her attention on a light-haired woman wearing a blouse that barely covered her shoulders. Maybe that one, she thought. Maybe that one is like my mother. Why, Emily wondered, was she always thinking about her mother? Perhaps, when she was older, she would make a trip back to the mining camps and find her. She would ask her if the rumors were true, and why she had chosen a life of ill repute over a life with her daughter.

"Emily?" Clay called.

She quickened her step to catch up with Clay and Betsy, but not until she looked one last time over her shoulder.

When they rounded the corner they were surrounded suddenly by a group of children dressed in rags. "Look at those poor little tykes," Emily said, tempted to give them part of her vanilla cake.

"They aren't so poor," Clay laughed. "That young one there is the mayor's son Tommy."

Laughing and running, the children costumed as orphans played kick-the-can. By the look on Betsy's face, it was very clear to Emily that Betsy wanted to join them. "Go ahead," Emily encouraged, remembering playing the same game with George and Lizzie only months ago in Saw Tooth City.

At first Betsy held back, shy, but with encouragement from Clay, Betsy ran forward and joined the children. When the can was kicked toward them, Clay, without reservation, kicked it to Emily.

Seeing his sheepish grin, Emily picked up her skirt and kicked the can so hard it flew through the air. Perhaps it was the heat, the confining corset. Or perhaps it was because she had moved too quickly, but Emily fell backwards, unable to catch her balance. She was sure she was going to ruin her new dress when Clay stepped forward to catch her.

"Emily," he said, "be careful."

He held her too long before he released her and for a moment, one fleeting minute, she wished he was the man who still owned her heart. Her first love was proving impossible to forget.

"They're having a giant picnic at the pavilion," he said, releasing her with some embarrassment. "Shall we get something to eat?"

Emily nodded, even though eating was the last thing she wanted to do.

* * *

The banquet hall was elegantly arranged with long tables heaped high with delicacies of the season. Flowering plants, fruits, and cut-glass dinnerware presented a beautiful appearance. The walls were hung with tricolored shields bearing the inscriptions *Vive la France! and Vive la République!* After sampling the delicious fare, the trio ambled through the grounds, stopping when they came to a large dancing pavilion. Clay turned to Emily and asked, "Would you care to dance?"

The music was inviting. But she had never danced the way these people did, moving elegantly around the pavilion. She only knew how to do reels, country dances. What if she missed a step? What if she tripped on her dress? She couldn't chance embarrassing him in front of all of these people.

"I'm sure Betsy would like to," she said, hoping to dissuade him.

Clay did not let her refusal dampen his spirits. He offered his arm to Betsy. "Little Bit, may I have the pleasure?"

Betsy giggled and followed him onto the dance floor. From where she stood Emily could watch them. He made it look so easy. In his arms, Betsy floated above the floor. She was laughing when they returned to Emily's side, her cheeks flushed with excitement.

"Now it's your turn, Miss Emily." Clay bowed and her heart caught. If only he didn't remind her so much of Kerry. If only she had met him first.

After an afternoon of dancing and amusements, and just before the sun set, they settled on the lawn to watch the display of fireworks. As Emily looked up at the nighttime sky, she compared the colorful explosions overhead to fireworks she had witnessed in Rocky Bar. The mining town was filled with gaiety, but the mountain sky, even with all of its million stars, was never this beautiful, not even when burnished gold by the Northern Lights. Emily watched the sky with wonder. St. Louis might be warmer, muggier than the mountains, but here the festivities felt much more civilized. Saw Tooth City and Rocky Bar seemed a million miles away.

Betsy's head began to nod. Emily pulled the child close. Without being asked, Clay offered his jacket as a pillow and turned his gaze to the sky. Because they sat so close Emily could smell him—the familiar scent of warm leather and soap. Between the colorful explosions, she watched the stars and made a wish. She glanced at Clay and wondered. Was he making one of his own?

"Time to go, sleepyhead." Clay leaned over to rouse Betsy.

"I'm awake." She rubbed her eyes.

"Well, then, I think it's time we headed home."

Home, Emily thought to herself, liking the way he said it. As if it were something permanent, just within her reach.

Clay helped Emily to her feet and the three of them walked toward the stables, where Jonathan waited with the carriage. But before they reached the carriage, they passed a large amphitheater where music spilled out into the night air.

"Let's go see." Betsy, now wide awake, pulled Emily toward the music. She didn't release Emily's hand until they had joined the crowd jamming the stage. And even though the notes drifting out over the crowd were lovely, they were also familiar. When a woman stepped on stage and began to sing, Emily didn't have to look up through the crowd to know who it was. She would recognize that voice anywhere.

CHAPTER TWENTY-ONE

"How do you like the Queen?" the Cat asked.
"Not at all," said Alice. "She's so extremely—" Just then she noticed that the Queen was close behind her, listening: so she went on, "—likely to win, that it's hardly worth while finishing the game."
ALICE IN WONDERLAND

AS EMILY WATCHED, Jenny moved across the stage singing lyrics Emily had heard before. She didn't want to stare, but it seemed to Emily that Jenny had grown thinner, so jaundiced even her greasepaint couldn't hide the fact that she was ill. Twice before the song was finished Jenny stopped to catch her breath, to cough into her handkerchief. And it could have been only her imagination, but Emily believed she saw blood when Jenny put her handkerchief away.

The red dress Jenny wore—the one Emily had tried on a lifetime ago in Vienna—seemed garish hanging from Jenny's thin shoulders. Emily thought she heard snickers along with the audience's cheers of "Brava!" when the song was finished. The music changed just then, and Emily turned her head in time to see the rest of the troupe—Bella, Brooks, and Ellerton—join Jenny on stage. Emily glanced around for Kerry, almost hoping he wouldn't appear. But like the accomplished artist he was, he didn't disappoint her. For there he was, promenading across the stage like Charles Dickens himself as he bowed to the audience and joined the others.

With a theatrical bow, Kerry took Jenny's hand and together the troupe sang "La Marseillaise." Several in the audience joined along with the chorus. Emily looked at Clay to see if he was singing, but he was silent, his face the color of granite.

"French national anthem," Clay explained, somewhat distracted when he caught her watching him. He returned his attention to the stage. He can't keep from staring at Jenny, Emily thought, no more than she could help glancing from time to time at Kerry. She'd heard the expression before, "he wears his heart on his sleeve," and when she looked at Clay she knew exactly what it meant. She didn't want to admit it, but she felt a little jealous. Even though at the same time she was watching Kerry, wishing her heart wasn't churning like butter. Even as she watched him lead the crowd jubilantly in song.

"Voient ton triomphe et notre gloire!" the troupe members sang, ending their show.

"We should go," Emily said, hoping to pull Clay and Betsy away before the troupe mingled with the crowd after the performance. As she tried to leave, though, they were stopped by another of Clay's acquaintances.

"Clayton. If you would please, a minute of your time."

"Judge Spencer." Clay offered his hand. "This is a surprise."

"Every now and then a man has to get out and see how the rest of the world lives," the judge said. "If I could have a word with you." The judge nodded briefly to Emily. "Ma'am."

"Miss McIntyre," Clay said, "if you'll excuse us." He followed the judge away from the crowd, where the two men conversed privately. Not eager to run into Jenny, or Kerry either for that matter, Emily led Betsy away from the amphitheater.

"We'll wait for your uncle here," she said to Betsy. Emily watched the troupe leave the stage and join the audience, which in its excitement pressed closer and closer, making it impossible for Emily and Betsy to exit without getting trampled. Glancing over her shoulder, she could see Clay and the judge deep in conversation. "It looks like your uncle may be a while," Emily said to Betsy. "Perhaps we should wait for him in the carriage."

Having made her decision, Emily tried to catch Clay's attention. But when she waved, it was Kerry who nodded, mistaking her greeting for him. Her hand turned to ice, and she wanted to bolt, to get as far away as possible. But it was too late. Kerry had already seen her, and it was clear he was making his way toward her even though he offered his hand and a smile to an occasional admirer along the way.

In the shadows cast by the gaslights he was still striking. She could see that his blond goatee was neatly trimmed as usual. She took a step backward as he approached, remembering how warm his lips felt when he kissed her, how she trembled when he untied her bonnet.

"Kerry Chapman," he said taking her hand into his. "At your service." And though he wore gloves, her hands burned where he touched hers.

"My, what a fine young lady you have here." He bowed to Betsy. "You must be a princess."

"I'm not a princess," Betsy giggled. "I'm Betsy."

"Betsy," he smiled. "Such a charming name." He turned his attention to Emily. "You have a fine looking daughter here, Mrs…"

With the blood rushing from her face, Emily found it hard to think. Was he mocking her, or had he truly not recognized her? She decided to play it straight. "McIntyre," she said.

"Mrs. McIntyre. It is a lovely evening we are having."

"It is," Emily managed to mumble.

"Well, Mrs. McIntyre. A pleasure to make your acquaintance. As well as that of your lovely daughter." He tipped his hat and pulled two tickets from his pocket. "We will be performing at Forest Park later this week. I hope you and your good husband will find time to attend. I couldn't have a beauty like you miss my show, now could I?" He smiled and she could see that his smile was artificial, part of his act. His teeth were crooked, even yellow, something she never noticed before. And the smell of his cologne did nothing to hide the fact that his jacket needed cleaning.

"Thank you." Emily held a handkerchief to her face. She accepted the tickets and wondered how she could have ever thought this man could be her only joy, her very life. She shuddered, knowing that just a few months ago she was willing to trade her future to be his wife.

"Mr. Chapman!" A group of admirers interrupted them. "We so enjoyed your show."

Kerry extended his hand to a young couple, and Emily saw her opportunity to leave. As she guided Betsy toward Clay, Emily fought the humiliation tearing in her eyes. She could blame the shadows, she thought, biting her lip. True, she had grown thinner, paler. She wore her hair up instead of down and was rarely seen without her corset—a corset he had purchased. But even if it were noon and the sun were overhead in a cloudless sky, she knew. The man who had once called her his own little Robin of the Rockies and paraded her down the streets of Ketchum wouldn't have recognized her, wouldn't have known she was willing to follow him all over the world, all for the price of a song.

Still clutching the tickets, Emily stood near the edge of the crowd searching for Clay.

"I'm sorry," he said, approaching with long strides. "I didn't mean to keep you waiting. You know business."

Emily knew nothing about business, but she knew this man. If he had seen Jenny, if he had spoken to Kerry, he would never tell her, of that she was sure. That and the fact that she wanted to leave the fairgrounds as quickly as possible. She was relieved when he offered his arm. "Shall we?"

Emily nodded. As they made their way toward the carriage, Emily slowly opened her hand and one by one let Kerry's show tickets fall to the ground.

Inside the carriage, Emily adjusted her new bonnet and leaned back in her seat. With her eyes closed, she could still see Kerry and Jenny. She was glad it was dark enough to hide her humiliation. What an innocent she had been, pining all this time for a man who didn't even recognize her, a man who didn't even remember her name.

Betsy's head bobbed against Emily's shoulder, and Emily slid over to make more room on the seat for the sleeping child. That, however, put Emily closer to Clay, and she tried not to bump into him every time the carriage swayed.

If he was bothered by their accidental contact, he didn't show it; he didn't move away. If anything, he seemed to draw closer, seemed almost sad when they reached the manor. "Thank you for a most enjoyable day," Clay said as he helped Emily from the carriage.

"It's I who should be thanking you. For a wonderful time and these lovely gifts."

They stepped to one side, out of Jonathan's way as he gathered Betsy and carried her into the house. Emily and Clay lagged behind as if each wished the evening didn't have to end. "It was all very exciting," Emily said. "A memorable outing."

"I'm glad you enjoyed it." Clay stopped before they reached the steps and reached for her hand, which he kissed so gently Emily thought she imagined his touch.

"I did." Emily reclaimed her hand, which, when touched by Kerry felt on fire, but when kissed by Clay felt light, as if it might float away.

He moved closer and for a moment Emily thought he was going to kiss her. "Forgive me," he said, backing away.

They walked up the steps to the house without sharing words, each contemplating their own expectations. And the reflection that bothered Emily the most was the one where she wondered if Clay wished the hand he'd kissed had been Jenny's instead of her own.

The next morning the house was astir. Mary trembled in the hallway while Mrs. Talbot raged. "I told you to keep that door locked. Now, something precious is missing."

What? Emily wondered as she sat down to breakfast. What was so important it had everyone walking on tiptoes and staring at the floor? The distress inside the house was so intense she decided to take Betsy outdoors and away from all the commotion. They were in the garden reading from *Alice in Wonderland* when Emily heard a rustle behind them. When she turned, Emily was stunned to see Jenny standing in the shadows.

Realizing she had been discovered, Jenny stepped forward. "Look at you," Jenny whispered. "You look well."

Emily couldn't say the same about Jenny. Her eyes were hollow, dark and dull. An odor Emily recognized as the lingering smell of sickness replaced the fragrance of gardenias that used to follow Jenny like honeybees. Even the garden roses couldn't mask the offensive odor.

"What do you want?" Emily stood, making sure there was a safe distance between Jenny and Betsy.

"I wanted to see . . ." Jenny still wore the locket on a chain around her neck. She resorted to her old habit of touching it every few minutes when she was nervous.

An awkward silence passed, filled with too many things unsaid, until Emily placed a protective hand on Betsy's shoulder. "Little Bit," she said, "go inside."

"Wait." Jenny stepped forward and addressed Betsy. "What a lovely dress you have. Did your mother make that for you?"

Betsy looked at Emily. "No," she said shyly.

"Such a pretty dress requires just the right accessories, don't you think?" Jenny removed her locket and without looking at Emily for approval, placed it around Betsy's neck. "There." She adjusted Betsy's collar. "That looks lovely."

"Can I keep it?" Betsy looked to Emily for approval.

Remembering the fuss Mrs. Talbot made over her dress, Emily wondered if they should refuse Jenny's gift. But, Emily reasoned, this was a gift between family members, so it must be proper for Betsy to accept. Besides, she had no right to prevent a gift between a mother and daughter. "It's very pretty," Emily said, and Betsy smiled.

"Thank you," Betsy said with a curtsey.

"You're welcome." Jenny bent down and offered her hand. "I'm happy to have made your acquaintance." She stood and challenged Emily in a broken whisper Betsy could not hear. "Take good care of my daughter." Before Emily could respond, Jenny faded back into the shadows, like a candle slowly snuffing out.

"Do you know that lady?" Betsy asked, trying to hold the locket for a better look.

"I met her once. A long time ago." Emily pretended to look at the sky. "Perhaps we should go inside."

"She's pretty," Betsy said, following Emily indoors. "But not as pretty as you."

* * *

They were in the middle of the evening meal when Clay noticed the locket. "Little Bit." He laid his fork on the table. "Where did you get that necklace?"

"From that nice lady," Betsy said.

"What nice lady?" Clay looked to Emily for an answer.

"Jenny." Emily's voice broke. "She was here."

"Here? At this house?" He didn't give her time to reply. "When?"

"This afternoon, sir." She wished now she had made Betsy return it.

He looked at Mrs. Talbot. The housekeeper made it sound like Emily was lying. "If she was here, sir, I didn't see her. No one's been near the house all day."

"What did she want?" he asked Emily.

"I—I'm not sure. She was only here a moment. Just long enough to leave the locket. I'm sure she meant no harm." Emily said it with conviction, knowing that earlier she herself was unsure of Jenny's motives.

"You should have told me." Clay pushed away his plate and rose. "In the future," he said to Emily, "I expect to be informed."

"Yes, sir." She looked at her plate, glad the meal was almost finished.

Emily was on her way to the library when she overhead the housekeeper and Clay talking. She stopped beside the door to listen. "We've looked high and low, sir. We can't find it anywhere," Mrs. Talbot said.

"Did you ask Betsy?"

"Yes, sir. And she doesn't have it."

"Well, keep looking. It's bound to show up somewhere."

When they vacated the room, Emily sat down with her book and began to read. But she couldn't keep her mind on the story. The antics of Pip and Estella seemed trivial compared to the tension plaguing Lafayette Manor. After her trying day, she decided to retire.

Upstairs, the door to her room was ajar. The few things she owned were in disarray. The bed had been stripped. Mrs. Talbot stood beside the bed, her arms crossed, her face rigid with anger. The contents of Emily's tin were strewn across the mattress.

The minute Emily entered the room, Mrs. Talbot picked up the ruby ring and accused her. "And how do you explain this? I knew it was you who took it all along. If you were an honest person, you would have said so this morning and saved us all this trouble."

Emily looked from the housekeeper to the ring. "I didn't take it."

"No, I suppose you didn't put it inside this box and hide it under the dresser where you thought no one would look, either, did you?" Mrs. Talbot's face was distorted with anger and hate.

Emily looked at the dresser, now pulled away from the wall, and all but upended. Mrs. Talbot had been very thorough in her search.

Almost as if she was aware of the tin box and unwilling to stop searching until she found it.

Clutching the ring, the housekeeper moved toward the door. "Wait till Mr. Morrison hears about this."

"Hears about what?" Betsy said from the doorway with a yawn.

Mrs. Talbot made a fist around the ring and set her lips. "None of your business. Shouldn't you be in bed?"

Betsy entered the room. "I heard all the yelling." She looked from Emily to the housekeeper. "What do you have in your hand?"

Mrs. Talbot opened her fist. "Your grandmother's ruby ring. It looks like Emily stole it," she said spitefully.

Betsy took the ring and slipped it on her finger. "Emily doesn't steal."

"That's for your uncle to decide." Mrs. Talbot said. "Once I tell him where I found it. Now give me the ring and go back to bed."

Betsy moved closer to Emily. Emily held out her hand and Betsy dropped it into her palm. "I know you didn't take it. Mrs. Talbot was looking at it. She said she was going to put it in a safe place."

Emily and Mrs. Talbot exchanged a knowing look. "Off to bed." Emily swatted Betsy's bottom. "I'll be in shortly."

When they were alone, Emily turned in the doorway. "Are you going to tell me Betsy is lying?"

"No." Mrs. Talbot stood rigid.

"Then," Emily offered the ring. "I think this should be returned to its rightful place, don't you? Somewhere safe?"

Mrs. Talbot snapped up the ring and charged out of the room, leaving Emily to clean up the mess.

CHAPTER TWENTY-TWO

She raised me, sat in her chair, and standing me before her, said, slowly, in a cold, low voice—I see her knitted brow, and pointed finger: —"Your mother, Esther, is your disgrace, and you were hers."
BLEAK HOUSE

EMILY WAS SITTING in a window nook of the parlor reading and Clay was tending to some legal documents, when Mrs. Talbot entered in a huff. "Mr. Morrison. If I may have a word with you."

Hidden by the curtain, Emily tipped her head, and Clay looked up. "What is it?"

"It's about that girl, sir." She spoke as if she couldn't bring herself to say Emily's name, as if she would burn a hole in her tongue if she said it aloud. Standing tall with her hands folded firmly in front of her, Mrs. Talbot continued. "I think you will be interested in seeing this letter that was delivered with yesterday's post." The housekeeper pulled an envelope from her apron pocket and placed it on the desk.

"That girl," Clay said, "has a name, Mrs. Talbot. Her name is Emily, and I wish you would stop finding ways to discourage rather than encourage her acceptance here at Lafayette Manor."

"You'll beg my pardon, sir. After you read that letter you won't want that imposter in this house, let alone near our Betsy."

The tops of Emily's ears burned, and it wasn't due to the morning sun streaming in the window. She laid down her book and stepped forward. "Who do you think I'm pretending to be?"

Emily's sudden appearance unsettled the housekeeper and she wrung her hands and sniffed. Shoulders back, chin set and eyes focused straight ahead, Mrs. Talbot left the parlor without looking at Emily.

When she was gone, Clay picked up the envelope. He turned it over. "It's from a Mrs. Gideon Harmon in Saw Tooth City. Shall we see what she has to say?"

"No." Emily said it so quickly he seemed startled. "I mean, yes, of course, by all means."

Setting the letter aside, he motioned to a chair. "You look pale, Emily. Please sit down." When she was settled he said, "Shall I ring for tea, some water?"

"No. I don't want any tea." What she'd really like to have said was *I'm sick to death of your tea, the Eastern attitudes cluttering this house like rubbish*. Instead, she leaned back in her chair and breathed as deeply as her confining corset would allow.

"So," he said, his hands folded on the desk tapping his thumbs together as if counting the seconds. "If I were to read this letter, what would I find? Would Mrs. Harmon say that you abused her children and neglected your duties?"

She looked up, startled. She did not remember discussing the Harmons with him. "No, I don't think so." She had no idea what Mrs. Harmon had written, but one thing was certain, it wouldn't be kind. At its very best it might accuse her of stealing money; at worst it might reveal the truth about her past and her mother.

"If I read it, will I discover that you have no scruples, that you put your needs above those of others?"

"Of course not," she said, looking down at her hands. What a silly question. How many months had she been in this house, two, three? Long enough for him to know that she minded her own business as she looked after Betsy.

"Will I read that you intend to steal me blind the minute my back is turned, or to spread vicious rumors?"

"No, sir."

"Will I learn that you fabricated the truth about your relatives? That you know no one in St. Louis besides the people who reside in this household?"

If humiliation were a color, it would have been red, because that was the color her face turned at his disclosure.

"Perhaps." She looked at the floor, ashamed and disgraced.

"Then," he said, tearing the letter in half and dropping it into the wastebasket, "I see no reason to read it. Don't you agree?"

"I…" If she were brave enough, she would tell him the truth. That way, the next time a threatening letter found its way into his hands, he wouldn't have to read it, he wouldn't be compromised.

"I think we are done here." He picked up his pen and turned back to his work.

Emily waited until she was sure her legs would hold her. Then she made her way toward the door. Before she could leave the room, Clay said without looking up from his work, "I'm here, Emily, should you need legal counsel."

She nodded, grateful he had his back to her and couldn't see the way her hands trembled, the way her fingers faltered at the door.

Instead of returning to her room or Betsy, Emily watched the parlor door closely, waiting for him to leave. When he did, she rushed into the parlor and reclaimed the torn letter. Alone in her bedroom, she opened the envelope, matched up the torn edges, and began to read. Along with a letter from Mrs. Harmon indicating that Emily left suddenly and ungratefully leaving her in a bind with spring chores to tend to, there was a newspaper clipping about a fire in Atlanta. Apparently caused by an overturned lantern, the fire had burned quickly, destroying most of the two-story building in minutes. Among the dead was Emily's mother, a known prostitute in the mining camp. There was even a picture of Emily's mother, before the fire. Emily stared at the picture and tried not to cry.

How many times had she lied and said her mother was dead? Her hand trembled. Seeing it in black and white made it final, and she fought the emotions conflicting inside her. Anger, because her mother died a fallen woman, but also sorrow and regret because now, at least for her mother, there was no time for remorse or redemption. Emily could no longer hope that her mother was still alive, longing to see her, or living a better life far from Idaho Territory. Emily read the clipping one more time before slipping it back into the torn envelope. She gently placed it inside her tin box next to her mother's silver brooch.

A wind came up, blowing rain against her window. The gloomy weather did nothing to help Emily's growing melancholia. Feeling blue, she thought she might have been better off drowning in the

Mississippi River. Then she wouldn't have had to feel the pain, the emptiness that came from having no living relatives, no father or mother.

Deciding nothing was gained by brooding, Emily resolved to lift her spirits by helping Mrs. Koch, knowing she could always find solace in the big kitchen. But when she punched down the bread dough so hard the table wobbled, Mrs. Koch scolded. "Not so vigorous. You'll make it tough." Shooing Emily aside with a swish of her hip, Mrs. Koch demonstrated. "Like this child, gentle."

Emily followed the cook's example, kneading the bread in between sighs.

"What's ailing you, child? You act like you lost your own mother."

That comment brought tears to Emily's eyes and she swiped at her face, leaving behind a trail of flour. "Nothing."

"Don't 'nothing' me. I know better. If it was nothing, you'd be romping with Betsy instead of moping around a kitchen with an old lady. Spill the beans. What's got you so down you're ruining my bread dough with all of your blubbering?"

That only made Emily cry harder.

"Now, now, now." Mrs. Koch steered Emily to a chair. "Sit yourself down." She walked across the room and closed the door, insuring their privacy. "Is it man trouble what's bothering you, child? I know a lot about man trouble."

"No," Emily said. "Not man trouble."

The cook looked at Emily with skepticism. "You aren't troubling yourself over Mr. Clay, now are you?" She didn't give Emily time to answer, but continued. "'Cause if you are, you're wasting your time acting like a lovesick puppy. He thinks very highly of you." She nodded matter-of-factly, filling the kettle with water and lighting the stove. "I can tell by the way he consults with you on Betsy's activities. But 'specially the way he asks after your well-being."

"It has nothing to do with Mr. Morrison," Emily said drying her eyes. "It's just that I—I received some bad news and I'm afraid it's made me melancholy."

"My mama always said misery loves company." The cook stepped into the pantry and returned with a jar of green leaves. "Sometimes it helps to talk it out."

Maybe it would, Emily thought. She'd gone all these months avoiding the truth, avoiding telling Clay about her background. Now she didn't have to tell him. It wasn't like he could run into her mother someday on the street, not now.

"Ay-yi-yi," Mrs. Koch cried, rushing to the water boiling over on the stove. While Emily grabbed a towel to mop up the floor, Mrs. Koch measured tea into a strainer and covered it with hot water. Satisfied with its strength, she poured Emily a cup and pushed it toward her, as if nothing had happened, as if the water in the kettle had never boiled over and there wasn't a huge mess to clean up. "Drink," she said. "It'll make you feel better."

Believing nothing would ever make her feel better again, Emily took a sip and recognized the flavor. Catnip to calm her nerves.

"You're wrong about Mr. Clay," the cook said looking at Emily evenly. "A fairer man you'll never find. He's not quick to judge. Besides, he has a special place in his heart for you."

"Even if that were true," Emily said, looking into her cup as if she could find absolution there along with the catnip, "there are some things a man can't abide. Like fallen women."

"What's that you say?" Mrs. Koch stared at Emily as if she couldn't believe her ears. "I've seen fallen women before, and you certainly are not one of them. Where did you get such foolishness?"

"Not me," Emily said, feeling the heat rise in her face. "My mother." There, it was out; there was no taking it back. She might as well march upstairs and pack her bag—no, Jenny's bag, she thought with disgust. Fifteen years old and she didn't even own her own satchel.

If she thought Mrs. Koch would go running from the room in horror, she was mistaken. Instead, the cook tipped Emily's face until she could look directly into her eyes. "You are not your mother."

"But Mrs. Talbot—"

"Forget Mrs. Talbot."

"She keeps asking for references, about my background. If she tells Mr. Morrison what she knows, he will never let me see Betsy again." Emily raised her gaze to meet Mrs. Koch's. "I made a promise to take good care of Betsy. I would like to keep it."

"Listen, child." The cook refilled their cups and settled into the chair beside Emily. "You're going to have to learn to trust someone.

Or else you're going to end up like Mrs. Talbot. Never been married, hard as nails, and more bitter than quinine."

"Never been married?"

"Never been married and that is part of what makes her so miserable. Hear tell she had an offer once a long time ago. But she didn't think she loved the man so she gave him the mitten and has been alone ever since." Mrs. Koch looked toward the closed door and continued. "Some women get the fool idea in their heads that they have to be falling down drunk with love before they can marry a man. But I think it's better to marry an honest man, one who's concerned with your welfare. Like Mr. Clay." She looked at Emily. "A body could do worse."

Emily ignored her implication. "If she's never been married, how can she call herself Mrs. Talbot?"

"Child, this is St. Louis. You can call yourself whatever you want and nobody's going to care."

"Mrs. Talbot's going to care once she learns the truth about my mother." Emily looked toward the door, afraid it would open any minute and her secret would be revealed to the rest of the household.

"That's why it's up to you to tell him first, before she can distort the facts and make it sound worse than it is."

As if it could get any worse, Emily thought, draining her cup. She hadn't planned on getting attached to Betsy or to Clay. Her plans had been to find work outside the house and away from them as soon as possible. But now she cared about them. Deeply.

"If we don't get back to that bread, we're going to have more than one mopey face around this house. And one is all I care to handle." Mrs. Koch gave Emily a smile as she carried their cups to the sink. Returning to her bread dough, she punched it down, covered it with a towel, and said, "You run along now. Mr. Clay is usually at his desk this time of day.

"Wait." Mrs. Koch arranged several slices of fresh bread on a tray along with butter and a hot pot of tea. "Take this into the parlor and tell him."

She could refuse, Emily thought, but where would that get her? That would only delay the inevitable. Clay might not have read yesterday's letter, but she was sure Mrs. Talbot had, that she was biding her time, waiting for the perfect opportunity to disgrace Emily's reputation. With a nervous look toward the parlor, Emily picked up the tray and pushed open the door.

As predicted, Clay was busy at his desk, writing furiously, when Emily entered. He looked up when he heard her step. "Emily?"

"Mrs. Koch thought you might enjoy some tea."

He put down his pen. "Why didn't she send Mary?" He stood and helped her settle the tray on the table. "She shouldn't have imposed on you. I will have to have a word with her."

"Oh, no. Please don't," Emily said, her voice unsteady. "I offered. Please don't scold her."

"I'll let it go this time. But I won't have her treating you like a common servant."

"Yes, sir." Emily looked toward the door, wondering if she still had time to change her mind.

"Come," he said. "Join me."

She wasn't hungry, or thirsty either for that matter. Her earlier cups of tea had left a bitter taste in her mouth, so sour she was sure even Mrs. Harmon's coffee could not purge the unpleasant flavor. But she knew she must come clean with him, so she poured them both a cup of tea. "I have something to tell you," she began.

Taking a drink, he set down his cup and gave her his full attention. "I hope you're not going to tell me you are leaving. I was completely out of line the other night. I am sorry if it has made you uncomfortable." He paused as if weighing his words. "Both Betsy and I think very highly of you. We would never want to give you cause for embarrassment."

Taking a deep breath to steady her voice, Emily said, "This has nothing to do with the other night. This is about me. When you hear what I have to say, I'm sure you will ask me to leave straight away."

Clay leaned back in his chair and studied her with his gray eyes. Uncomfortable under his even gaze, Emily rose and paced the room. "You have been very patient with me. I am not proud of what I have to tell you. But I feel I would be doing you a disservice if I keep silent any longer." She stopped pacing and looked at him directly. "Excuse me for a moment. I'll be right back."

Emily returned with the clipping and torn letter as proof. "Here." She handed him the article about the fire. "Maybe this will help explain. I hope you'll forgive me for opening a letter that was not addressed to me, but I had to know."

She watched as Clay scanned the clipping and reached the end of the story.

"That was my mother." Her legs became unsteady and she had to sit down. She expected him to be shocked, to be angry with her for keeping such a disagreeable secret. She couldn't be sure, but she thought the color of his eyes might have turned darker when he glanced at the letter.

It took some time for him to respond and when he did his voice was even, true to his profession, without emotion. "Why are you telling me this now?"

"Because I don't want to compromise this house, sir, or you or Betsy," she said, looking at the floor.

"But you were willing to do so before?"

She felt like a mouse caught in a trap. Nothing she said was going to make up for her silence. "I wasn't thinking clearly before," Emily said. "I was only trying to get away. I will go now." She started to gather the empty plates and cups to return them to the kitchen.

"Leave them," he said. "Sit down."

Her hands shook; she sat but began to sputter. "I will leave today. I will find a way to repay you."

"You'll do no such thing," he said. "I won't have you breaking Betsy's heart. I won't have another woman abandon her." He gave her back the clipping. "How could you possibly think I wouldn't know?"

She looked at him blankly. *He knew?* She shifted in her seat. Of course he would know. She hadn't thought so before, when he agreed to help her leave Idaho Territory, but he'd had several months to check up on her, several months in which to check her references. He might have even gone searching for her kin when she had been so sick. She felt stupid and immensely weary. "I'm sorry to disappoint you, sir." She looked at her hands, folded tightly in her lap.

He sounded tired, as though he had argued his case too long before the jury. "You haven't disappointed me, Emily. If anything, you have brought life back into this dreary house. You shouldn't be held responsible for your parents' shortcomings."

"But I am—"

"Only a child yourself."

"I am not a child," she said. "I've chopped down trees, put out kitchen fires. I've tended George and Lizzie since they were babies."

He started to laugh, and that made her even angrier. "I don't see anything to laugh about," she said.

"You wouldn't, my dear," he said. "You wouldn't." He rose and put his arm around her shoulder. "Do you think we can put an end to this unpleasant conversation now? Do you think we can go on about our business as usual without all the drama?"

She let him guide her to the door, thinking he must have lost his mind. But then, so had she, believing he would keep her in the house an hour longer than he had to. If she learned anything from Kerry Chapman it was this. Men couldn't be trusted, especially when their eyes were laughing.

CHAPTER TWENTY-THREE

...Charles Darnay seemed to stand in a company of the dead.
Ghosts all!...the ghost of youth, the ghost of age, all waiting their dismissal
from the desolate shore, all turning on him eyes that were changed
by the death they had died in coming there.
A TALE OF TWO CITIES

TWO DAYS PASSED and Clay never mentioned the article or Emily's mother, either. He hadn't asked her to leave, yet Emily was always watchful for some sign, some indication as to what he was thinking, what, if anything, he had told the household staff. In the meantime, she continued entertaining Betsy.

"That's not right," Betsy said when Emily tried to pronounce the French word for friend. "Like this, *l'ami.*"

"La ah me," Emily said, sending Betsy into circles with laughter. But they both stopped laughing when Clay entered the room, a copy of the *Post-Dispatch* tucked under one arm. His face was gray, like the color of his eyes. When he looked at Emily and Betsy, he didn't see them.

"Uncle Clay?"

"Little Bit." He faltered and pulled her close, so close she wiggled to get free. "How would you like to go see the steamboats?" he said releasing her.

"Oh, I would," she said. "Emily too?"

"Not this time," he said without looking at Emily. "This time I want it to be just me and you."

Emily could feel her face blaze. So there it was. He no longer wanted to be seen with her in public. As soon as a new companion for Betsy could be found, he would send her packing.

"Excuse me." Emily stood. "I have some mending to see to." She closed the book and slipped quickly from the room. She waited until she saw them drive away in the carriage, then returned to the library and took a book from the shelf. There on the desk was the newspaper, as Clay had left it.

POPULAR PERFORMER FOUND DEAD

Her book fell to the floor as Emily stared at Jenny Starr's picture, the same picture Emily had seen on posters advertising "The Kerry Chapman Troupe, the finest show west of the Mississippi." The same picture Emily carried for weeks in her apron pocket back in Saw Tooth City. Mesmerized, she read:

This morning the popular performer Jenny Starr was found dead in her room at the National Hotel. Miss Starr has long been known for her beauty and her entertaining voice. She had recently returned from a tour in the West to take part in St. Louis' Bastille Day festivities, where she gave a grand performance. The coroner said foul play is not suspected, that the woman was suffering many ailments considering the number of empty bottles found on a bedside table near the body. According to her manager, Mr. Kerry Chapman, the unfortunate songbird had been ill for several weeks.

A graveside service will be held later this week at Bellefontaine Cemetery, where Miss Starr will be interred.

Emily leaned back in her seat. Only last week . . .

She recalled the first time she had seen Jenny, covered with dust from the mining roads, and the way they had laughed when Jenny was laid up with her foot, the way Emily had adjusted the curls around Jenny's face before each performance. And now, Emily stared at the obituary, Jenny was dead.

Stunned, Emily sat for a long time trying to comprehend what she had read, brushing unconsciously at the tears on her cheek. *Betsy*, she thought, *oh, Betsy*.

Folding the paper so Jenny's picture was on the inside, Emily laid the paper on the table and retreated to Betsy's bedroom, where she crawled onto the child's bed, pulled Mr. Ears close, and began to rock with the rabbit. She didn't cry, not until she tried to sing "Songs My Mother Taught Me," and then it was a long time before she could stop crying.

She was reading in the parlor when Clay and Betsy returned later that afternoon.

"Emily," Betsy said, still excited from her outing. "Look what I got."

"Let's see," Emily said. "Would you look at that. Your very own paddleboat."

Betsy pulled a string and a whistle on the toy boat blew *toot-toot*. "Watch. It even makes steam," Betsy said.

"Quite remarkable." Fortunate child, Emily thought, until she remembered the news about Jenny.

"Do you want to see how it works?"

"Not now," Emily said. "I need to speak with your uncle."

"Alice?" Betsy called out as she ran from the room. "Look at my new boat."

Emily waited until they were alone before she asked him. "Will you go to Jenny's funeral?"

He seemed distracted. "Yes."

"Will you take Betsy with you?"

"No." He crossed the room to the liquor cabinet, poured himself a brandy, and drank half of it down.

"Without meaning to sound imprudent, sir, I think you should take her."

"It's not in her best interest." With one gulp he drained his glass.

"She has a right to know."

"I'll tell her when she's older. Right now it would only confuse her." He poured himself another drink and slumped into a chair. She'd never seen him so distraught. Still, she persisted.

"She's old enough to understand. Better to tell her now than to let her wonder all her life what she did to drive her mother away."

"She deserves better," he mumbled, emptying his glass.

"She has better," Emily said, standing close enough she could smell his brandy. "She has you."

When he looked up at her, his face was marked with pain and confusion. "If I take her," he hesitated, "—and I'm not saying that I will—will you come with us?"

"Yes," Emily said, taking his hand in hers. "Of course I will."

Later that night, after they had eaten and the house was quiet, she found Clay in the library, staring blankly at the unlit fireplace.

"If you approve, sir, I would like to make Betsy a dress for the funeral."

"That isn't necessary," Clay said without looking her way. "I'll send for the dressmaker."

"I can sew," Emily said. "I want to do this." She was feeling restless again, out of place. Keeping her hands busy would keep her out of trouble, keep her from thinking about her increasing feelings for Clay and Betsy. "Please, sir."

He shook his head no until he saw the hopeful expression on her face. "Very well. I will order the material tomorrow. And Emily," he added almost as an afterthought, "Thank you."

"You're welcome." She left the room knowing her offer wasn't much, but at least in her own simple way she could be of some help now when he needed it the most.

She kept busy, preparing a pattern until the fabric arrived. Then, after cutting and sewing, she pulled the new dress over Betsy's head and said, "Hold still or I'll stick you." While Betsy squirmed, Emily pinned the hem on the black dress in place. "That should do it. Now, young lady, if you will be so kind as to take that off, we'll get it hemmed."

"Emily?" Betsy seemed pensive as she let Emily pull the dress up over her head.

"What is it?"

"Are you coming with us?"

"I am."

"Do you know who died?"

"I do," Emily said. "Don't you?"

"No," Betsy said. "But I heard Mary say it was one of our relatives."

Curse him, Emily thought, sitting down with needle and thread. He wasn't going to tell her. She threaded the needle, tied a knot, and pulled it tight. With each additional stitch she took she grew angrier. Very well, she thought as she sewed. *Then I will.*

She decided to tell Betsy after dinner, but the right time never seemed to arise. Later, in Betsy's bedroom snuggled atop Betsy's bed with a book, Emily finished reading the story and closed the book. "Betsy," she began, but faltered when the child yawned and burrowed under her blanket. Resolve was strong until it came face to face with truth, and then it fell apart, she discovered. She couldn't tell Betsy before she went to bed. She couldn't send Betsy to sleep with a million questions and misgivings. No. She would wait for a better time. Perhaps in the morning. "Good night," she said to Betsy. "Pleasant dreams."

"Good night," Betsy answered, then rolled over and closed her eyes. Emily watched as Betsy slept, knowing that soon the child's world would splinter forever.

When morning came there was no time, no time that seemed right to tell Betsy. Dressed in their funeral clothes, Emily, Clay, and Betsy rode to the cemetery in silence. She should have found a time to tell Betsy, Emily thought, disgusted with her lack of action. For all her resolve and good intentions, she wasn't any braver than her employer.

She was surprised to see so few people at the service. She didn't expect to see Clay's father; he'd made it quite clear he wouldn't come. But after reading the notice in the *Post-Dispatch* she had expected to see more in attendance, if only to satisfy their curiosities about the famous Jenny Starr. Emily studied the crowd, recognizing Bella, Ellerton, and Brooks standing off by themselves in a corner. Kerry was nowhere to be seen, and for that she was grateful. She was having a hard enough time controlling her emotions in front of Betsy without having to deal with her feelings for him. She let her mind wander to happier times and wasn't aware that the prayer was over until she heard the minister say, "Amen."

"Amen," she mimicked, and soon Emily, Clay, and Betsy were the only ones left standing near the freshly dug grave. Each of them held a single red rose. Without words Emily led Betsy forward.

"Rest in peace, Jenny." Emily placed her rose on the grave.

"Rest in peace." Betsy followed Emily's example.

Clay laid his rose next to theirs. Then he turned to Emily and Betsy. "We should go."

"Not yet," Emily said. "Betsy, come here."

She was grateful she had had no time for breakfast, for if she had, she knew she would not be able to keep it down now as she bent beside the child. "I have something I need to tell you." She took a deep breath to steady her nerves. "Do you remember who this woman was?"

"Yes," Betsy said. "We saw her sing at the park." Her hand moved to the locket around her neck. "She gave me this."

"Yes, she did." Emily looked directly at Clay, daring him to stop her. But he stood silently behind Betsy, his hands on her shoulders.

"This is a secret locket." Emily pushed a lever and the locket sprang open. "See here? This is Jenny. Before she was famous."

"She was pretty," Betsy said.

"Yes, she was. And look here." Emily turned the locket so they could see the picture on the opposite side. Who do you think this little girl looks like?"

Betsy studied the picture for a while before said, "Miss Starr when she was a baby?"

"That's a good guess," Emily said. "But look at the nose. Doesn't it look just like a little girl named Betsy?"

"No." Betsy looked at the picture, then up at Emily with a question. But instead of asking Emily, she turned to her uncle and said, "Uncle Clay?" His jaw was set, and Emily could see he was having a hard time holding in his emotions. The only one calm was Betsy, and she couldn't seem to fathom why they were making such a fuss.

He offered his hand and said, "Come. Let's take a walk."

Confused, Betsy looked at Emily, and Emily nodded. "I'll be right over there if you need me." She turned and walked away from the grave before Betsy could see her tears.

When Emily felt she was at a safe distance for the two of them to talk in private, she slowed her step and looked back over her shoulder. Clay had pulled Betsy up onto his lap, and they had their heads bent together, like conspirators of a deep, dark secret. She wondered what he would tell her—if he would tell Betsy the truth about her mother. Or would he be kind and let her believe Jenny was a great songstress, loved and admired by people all over the world? What purpose would it serve to have Betsy know Jenny was addicted to fame, drugs, men, and money? That she may have had a beautiful voice, but had no skills as a mother?

What purpose, exactly, Emily thought, wandering through the cemetery while she waited. None whatsoever. The truth would only make the abandonment harder to bear. Why not, for the sake of

Betsy's future, leave the past where it belonged? Why not indeed, Emily thought as she studied the graveyard. Many secrets lay there, as well they should.

As Emily walked, she examined the headstones. She stopped before a large marble memorial and read:

SACRED
TO THE MEMORY OF
DR. WILLIAM NAYLOR
WHO DEPARTED THIS LIFE APRIL 25, 1853
AGED 68 YEARS
WHERE IMMMORTAL SPIRITS REIGN,
THERE WE SHALL MEET AGAIN

She stopped at another and read:

SAMUEL LAMBERT
DIED
April 13, 1881
Aged 52 Years

Beside this grave was another with a smaller headstone:

EVELEEN LAMBERT
Beloved Daughter of
SAMUEL & JANE A. LAMBERT
Died Sept 11th 1879
Aged 6 Years
Gone, but not forgotten

Emily let her hand trace the child's name, Eveleen. Who were these people, she wondered. Where did they come from—what had become of their families? She thought of her own dead mother and, still weepy from Jenny's service, let the tears roll down her face, never before realizing how hard it was to let go of a dream. When she returned to Lafayette Manor, she would put away her tin box and her dreams of finding her mother and concentrate on being a good companion to Betsy. She would keep her promise to Jenny.

Her tears dried as she walked through the parklike cemetery with its well-kept lawns. She was ready to turn back when she noticed an area beyond the massive iron gate outside the cemetery to what appeared to be a sadder, smaller plot, where weeds grew tall and graves stood untended. It reminded her of the Chinese graves back in Rocky Bar, and she wondered whether anyone left offerings at these graves to keep those in the afterlife from being hungry or lonely. Perhaps she would find an orange, a bowl of rice, or a cup of tea if she looked. Emily grew homesick remembering how she, George, and Lizzie had crept among the Chinese graves, daring one another to steal oranges, only to put them back before they dared eat them, unwilling to make the Chinese spirits angry.

Venturing closer, Emily noticed that here the tombstones were less ornate, the inscriptions modest. Some graves bore no markers at all. She paused and turned her head toward the Pacific Ocean and wondered if anyone bothered to mark the spot where her mother laid buried, back in Atlanta. For a fleeting moment she wanted to run home, back to Idaho Territory, and find out. But that was unrealistic if not impossible.

She continued through the modest cemetery until she came upon a section where all the headstones were plain, or had a single inscription, UNKNOWN. She shivered as the air grew colder, feeling as if the sun had been banished from this part of the cemetery. She glanced up, expecting to see a cloudy sky, but the sky was clear. Wishing she had thought to bring along a shawl, she turned, eager to return to her employer and Betsy.

As she made her way through the weeds and unmarked graves, she forgot to look for oranges, rice, or empty teacups. In her haste, her foot slipped, and she all but turned an ankle. Looking down, she saw an engraved stone half embedded in the dirt. She bent over to examine the stone, pushing aside a clump of nettle and read:

rah Ann
ied

How sad to have your gravestone broken, unmarked, so no one could find you. Emily searched for the other pieces, believing she was the reason the marker was shattered. She examined the ground until she found them. Brushing the dirt aside, she tried to fit the pieces together. There, she thought, that's better. But a chill settled over her, bringing her to her knees when she looked closer and read:

Sarah Ann McIntyre
Died November 17, 1879
Age Unknown

"Emily?" She could hear her employer calling, but she did not answer. She was too busy pulling weeds away from the grave. This wasn't her mother, of course, but it could be—sure as her name was Emily Ann.

"Emily?" called Clay again. "Ah, there you are. We should be going. It will be dark soon." Seeing her kneeling in the dirt, he asked, "What are you doing?"

Her mouth was dry. She couldn't speak. He stood directly over her and offered her a hand up. When she continued to work, he squatted down beside her. "We have to go."

She pushed his hand away and continued to pull at the weeds. "This is disgraceful." She worked harder, hoping someone back in Idaho Territory would be kind enough to occasionally see to the weeds growing around her mother's grave. She didn't care if Clay Morrison found her offensive, if he discarded her like a pitcher of soured milk. She wasn't leaving until every weed was gone. She worked harder, as if she had lost her senses, as if cleaning the gravesite would erase her past and change who she was.

"Here," he said. "Let me help." He bent down and helped pull nettle and burr from the overgrown site. As he worked, a briar caught the finger of his glove, ripping it in two. But that didn't stop him. Not even when he cut his finger and it began to bleed.

"I can help," Betsy said, pulling at weeds until her face was smudged. Seeing the child's eagerness to please made Emily's eyes tear all over again, and she pulled Betsy close for comfort.

"Ah, Little Bit," Emily said. "We make a sorry pair."

Clay tamped the headstone back together and centered it at the top of the grave. Like Betsy, he too, had soiled his clothes, and Emily expected him to stop there. Instead, he pulled branches from a dead willow nearby. He used his knee to snap them in pieces to make a boundary around the unkempt grave. "This will keep strangers from trespassing," Clay said as he worked. With Emily and Betsy's help, they labored until there was nothing else left to do.

Brushing the dirt from his clothes, Clay said, "We should hurry. They will lock the gates soon. Come, let's go home."

He said it like "home" was a word Emily knew, like she hadn't spent the better part of her life searching for a place to call home.

"Come." He offered his hand and helped her to her feet. "I'll take you home."

If only, Emily thought as she stepped into the carriage brushing at the threatening tears. If only that were true.

CHAPTER TWENTY-FOUR

"When I speak of home, I speak of the place where—in default of a better—those I love are gathered together; and if that place were a gypsy's tent, or a barn, I should call it by the same good name notwithstanding."
NICHOLAS NICKLEBY

THE RIDE BACK to the manor was marked with sadness and reflection. Betsy, the only one able to rest, leaned against her uncle. Her eyes threatened to close.

Staring out the carriage window, Emily watched the passing scenery. She had expected to be strong for Betsy. But she had failed. The child had turned to her uncle for comfort. So had Emily, as much as her pride would allow. She stared out at the hawthorn trees and wheat fields as they passed, the pink streaks in the sky, and saw further—mountains and streams, her father's grave atop a hill outside Rocky Bar, her mother's unmarked grave in a weed-infested field somewhere near Atlanta. And even though she sat close enough to Clay and Betsy to touch them, she had never felt so alone, or so discouraged. She had saved no one, not even herself.

As soon as the carriage stopped, Emily retired to her room and for the first time since she arrived at Lafayette Manor, locked her door. Brushing the dirt from her clothes, she knew she couldn't stay there. Perhaps, she thought, slowly packing her belongings, she could find a place somewhere between St. Louis and Idaho Territory, someplace she wouldn't feel so awkward or misplaced. A place where love couldn't be spoiled by leaving it out too long in the sun. A place she could call home.

Starting to pack her tin box into the satchel, she slumped to the floor, her mettle dulled to less than a strand of hair. Lifting the lid, she took out her mother's brooch and whispered, "Tell me, Mama, what should I do? Where shall I go?"

"Emily?" Mary, the kitchen maid, knocked at the door. "Dinner is served."

Emily stared at the door. "Tell Mrs. Talbot to begin without me."

"She'll be angry. You know she doesn't like to keep the family waiting."

Then she shouldn't have to worry, Emily wanted to say, because I'm not family. Instead, she bit her lip to keep still. Only when she was sure Mary was gone did she move quickly around the room.

With her belongings packed, Emily sat on the edge of her bed and considered returning to Saw Tooth City, to George and Lizzie and the closest thing she had to family. She could see them now, dangling their feet in Beaver Creek while Mrs. Harmon slept. No matter how hard she tried to see herself with her feet cooling beside theirs in the water, she could never accept their mother for her own. Nor their father.

She thought about George, about Lizzie, and wondered as they grew if they would become images of their parents. Would Lizzie bark orders, all the while gossiping cruelly about her neighbors? Would George trade his bow and arrow for a gun; would he be able to pull the trigger to gain another's fortune?

No. Even though their mother was a selfish busybody and their father was a profiteer, that didn't make George and Lizzie brutal, selfish children. On the contrary. She couldn't have asked for a more loving brother or sister, even if they didn't share the same last name.

Emily's thoughts settled on Clay. His father was the most cantankerous, bitter man Emily had ever had the privilege of sitting across the table from. But that didn't make Clay evil and selfish. In fact, Clay was the complete opposite of his father. She had never met a kinder, more considerate man.

She thought of Betsy and the grueling day she endured with barely a whimper. She wasn't a bad child. Bad behavior hadn't sent Jenny away. Greed and addiction drove Jenny from her home, from her daughter, and finally to her grave.

Holding her mother's brooch, Emily played with the clasp. Just because her mother was a fallen woman didn't mean Emily was too. Just because her mother left Emily behind didn't mean her mother didn't love her. Pinning her mother's brooch to her blouse, Emily whispered, "Watch me, Mama. Watch me. I will make you proud."

Satchel in hand, Emily picked up *Great Expectations*, the book she had borrowed from the library. She opened the door and made her way down the stairs. Leaving her satchel in the hallway by the front door she moved toward the library, intending to return the book before she left.

"They are expecting you," Mary whispered, passing Emily in the hallway with a tureen of soup. Emily took a deep whiff, and Mary nodded. "Yes'm, it is onion. Your favorite, at Mrs. Talbot's request."

Ready to bolt, Emily reconsidered. Every time she ran away, she only found herself in deeper trouble. She could pick up her satchel and run to the end of the world, but she could never run fast enough or far enough away to escape her past or her parentage. And in the other room waiting for her to join them for dinner was a family that needed, and some, like Betsy, who in their own way loved, her. They wouldn't turn her away. Hadn't they in fact sent Mary to fetch her for dinner? In spite of everything, they wanted her to stay.

Laying the book on her satchel, Emily turned toward the parlor and with each step she took, she thought hard. She'd find a way to win Mrs. Talbot's favor. Perhaps she'd ask Mrs. Koch when Mrs. Talbot's birthday was and braid her a pin from Betsy's hair. If she had already missed the housekeeper's birthday, Christmas was not too far away. She might even ask Mrs. Talbot to teach her French. In the meantime, she would do her very best not to upset the stern and lonely woman.

Emily took another step. She would keep her promise to Jenny. She would stay with Betsy. Long after she earned enough to repay Clay the money she owed him, long after she had enough money to be off on her own. She would stay as long as Betsy needed her.

Emily approached the dining room. Her stomach rumbled, reminding her that she had eaten nothing all day. The smell of onion soup and potato rolls lured her closer. She opened the door and walked in.

Mrs. Talbot looked up with distaste. "You are late. As you can see, we have started without you."

With a sincere smile, Emily nodded to Mrs. Talbot. "That's as it should be. I apologize for my bad manners. I will do my best to see that it doesn't happen again." She crossed the room to her chair but before she sat down she said to the head housekeeper, "Mrs. Talbot, everything looks lovely. Thank you so much for arranging such a pleasing table. And for the onion soup."

Chin set, Mrs. Talbot nodded.

As Clay held her chair, Emily looked at the people gathered around the table, this odd family. It had been a long time since she thought of Clay as David Copperfield. He was just a son trying to please an overbearing father and at the same time fulfill a promise to his dead brother.

She turned her attention to Betsy, who was never Little Nell at all, but Betsy, whom Emily had come to love like a sister, someone who loved books and boats as much as she did.

"Mary," Mrs. Talbot prompted the kitchen maid. "Bring Miss Emily some warm soup." The housekeeper met Emily's gaze, then turned back to her food.

Mrs. Talbot truly means no harm, Emily thought, dipping her spoon into the soup and savoring its richness. *This is all she has. Of course she wants to protect it.*

And Clay's father, Emily thought, daring to look his way tonight, on one of the rare nights he decided to join the family for dinner. He wasn't really like Ebenezer Scrooge at all, but rather a harmless old man trying too hard to hold on to his family as well as his business.

Clay passed the basket of potato rolls, and Emily selected a small one. She took a bite, enjoying the warm, floury flavor. She took another bite and this time, when she buried her teeth into the sweet warm bread, she did so as Emily Ann McIntyre, daughter of Steve and Sarah and not as Jenny Starr, Lucie Manette, or Alice chasing a white rabbit. This time she was content to enjoy her roll exactly as she was.

She passed the basket of rolls back to Betsy and looked up at Clay. Funny about life, she thought. You never know where it might lead you if you were only brave enough to follow.

Goldie's Daughter
DISCUSSION QUESTIONS

1. If Emily McIntyre hadn't chosen to leave Saw Tooth City, what would her options have been as a woman in a mining camp? What occupations were available to women in the 1880s?

2. Emily escapes the drudgery of her daily routine by reading books. What do you do to escape yours?

3. Like Emily, have you experienced situations in which your parents embarrassed you? If so, how? Have you ever wanted to run away from your heritage or change your name?

4. If Emily is so embarrassed by her mother, why is she driven to find out more about her?

5. Why is Emily drawn to Kerry Chapman? Have you ever encountered someone like Kerry Chapman? Do you still think about your first love?

6. Jenny Starr was beautiful and talented. Why do you think she became addicted to opiates?

7. Emily thinks that traveling with the troupe will be better than living in a mining camp. Compare her expectations with the reality. Have you ever achieved a dream that surpassed your expectations?

8. Compare Emily's life in Saw Tooth City to her life in St. Louis. How is it different? How is it similar?

9. What are the common bonds between Emily and Betsy that lead to their friendship?

10. How do you define home?

ACKNOWLEDGMENTS

I have gold fever. Credit the cabin I own in the mountains not far from the old mining camps Rocky Bar and Atlanta, Idaho. Over the years I've made many trips into those camps, gleaning stories like gold nuggets. I enjoy learning about the early pioneers and try to imagine life in the camps when the mines flourished. One name I heard over and over again was that of "soiled dove" Annie Morrow.

Born in 1858, Felicia Ann McIntyre, "Peg Leg Annie," was a reported camp prostitute whose feet froze in a snowstorm in 1896. Once I heard about Peg Leg Annie, I couldn't get her out of my head. What was it like growing up in a mining camp? What if your mother was the camp prostitute? These questions prompted me to write Emily's story, and about her quest to find a home and the truth about her mother.

Thanks to the many people who helped create this book. To my team at Booktrope: Kay Ellington, Barbara Brannon, Cindy Slator, and Greg Simanson, not to mention the superb support staff behind this team. To Sherri George and Dawn Blair, who for endless hours every week critiqued early drafts. To Patricia Santos Marcantonio, Dixie Thomas Reale, and Jennifer Sandmann, who read later drafts and commented on story and characters. To my readers Cheryl Maude and MaryAnn Runty. To my son, Trevor Dodge, the English professor who accomplishes what I can't, and last to my husband Paul, who transported me over those bumpy roads to Atlanta, Rocky Bar, Sawtooth City, and Vienna.

I thank you all from the bottom of my heart.

ABOUT THE AUTHOR

Bonnie Dodge was born in Jamestown, North Dakota, and grew up in Twin Falls, Idaho. She is author of *Miracles in the Desert,* a book of essays about Twin Falls, Idaho, and co-author to several *From the Snake River Plain* anthologies, as well as a young adult novel, *Billie Neville Takes a Leap*. Her fiction, poetry, and nonfiction have appeared in newspapers, magazines, and anthologies in the Pacific Northwest. Many of her short stories, poems, and essays have won awards, including the 2010 Idaho Writer's League Writer of the Year Award. Her novel *Waiting* was named Top Ten Idaho Fiction by Idaho Author Awards for 2014. She resides in Oregon and loves hearing from readers.

To find out more about Bonnie, visit her at:

facebook.com/BonnieDodgeAuthor

twitter.com/BJDodge

BonnieDodge.com

goodreads.com/author/show/6541864.Bonnie_Dodge

linkedin.com/pub/bonnie-dodge/65/8a7/2a3

MORE GREAT READS FROM BOOKTROPE

The Mind of a Child **by Marshanne Mishoe** (Contemporary Women's Fiction) Two eras, two women, one story of strength and love. *The Mind of a Child* paints a vivid picture of contrasting times, disparate perceptions, and the women who shaped them.

The Broken Half **by Sahar Abdulaziz** (Contemporary Women's Fiction) The harrowing story of a young American Muslim woman, Zahra, whose marriage has been anything but peaceful. Faced with difficult and dangerous choices, Zahra soon realizes each step to freedom is riddled with risky uncertainties.

Goddess of Suburbia **by Stephanie Kepke** (Contemporary Women's Fiction) Suburbia meets scandal in this hopeful and honest portrayal of that moment in every woman's life when it's time to make a change, even if that means risking losing it all.

The Paris Effect **by K.S.R. Burns** (Contemporary Women's Fiction) Love. Death. Paris. Food. Adventure. Betrayal. Escape. (Nothing is what it seems.) Dump your diet and escape to Paris in this quirky & highly praised debut novel!

Running Secrets **by Arleen Williams** (Contemporary Women's Fiction) Flight attendant Chris Stevens is bent on self-destruction until she meets Gemi Kemmal, an Ethiopian home healthcare provider. Together the women learn that racial identity is a choice, self-expression is a right, and family is a personal construct.

CPSIA information can be obtained
at www.ICGtesting.com
Printed in the USA
FSOW01n0702211215
14780FS

9 781513 703220